CROSSING THE LINE

Also by Bibi Belford
Canned and Crushed

CROSSING THE LINE

BIBI BELFORD

Sky Pony Press
New York

Sky Pony Press books may be purchased in bulk at special discounts for sales promotion, corporate gifts, fund-raising, or educational purposes. Special editions can also be created to specifications. For details, contact the Special Sales Department, Sky Pony Press, 307 West 36th Street, 11th Floor, New York, NY 10018 or info@skyhorsepublishing.com.

Sky Pony® is a registered trademark of Skyhorse Publishing, Inc.®, a Delaware corporation.

Visit our website at www.skyponypress.com.

10 9 8 7 6 5 4 3 2 1

Library of Congress Cataloging-in-Publication Data is available on file.

Cover illustration by Michael Lauritano
Cover design by Sammy Yuen

Print ISBN: 978-1-5107-0800-6
Ebook ISBN: 978-1-5107-0801-3

Printed in the United States of America

CROSSING
THE LINE

Chapter One

MY DA'S UNIFORM HANGS IN the closet, squeezed in between scratchy wool coats and my ma's ratty fur. He went straight to the hospital after the Great War. Never came home. When I press my nose to his brown jacket, I can't smell him anymore. Only mothballs. And ain't that just like life. Stinking stuff that overshadows all the good in the world.

When the Great War ended, people were happy. At first. But now things are going belly-up. Maybe all over the country, but Chicago, for sure, is in a fine kettle of fish.

The gangsters are shooting up the streets. Thugs like

Diamond Jim Colosimo and his wife's nephew, Papa Johnny Torrio, are getting away with murder. The police who shoulda been taking them down are running the numbers for the lawmakers, who are inviting the thugs to join their clubs and bring in votes.

President Wilson is off in France writing a peace treaty. The influenza epidemic is taking its toll on families already burdened with their soldier sons dying in the war, and every day trains full of migrating black Southerners are pulling into Chicago Central Station.

My friend Timmy's da come back from the war. Ready to roll up his sleeves and get back to work. But his job is gone. Given away to those Southerners.

Timmy's da is looking for a new job, but it's hard, Timmy tells me. His da's old boss at the steel mill ain't got nothing for him. So me and Timmy keep shining shoes at Central Station. Shining shoes for pennies that buy bread and sausage.

I feel safe and warm in the cave of coats, next to my da's uniform. Then the closet door opens and the light floods in on me. "Billy, Ma says to get ready for church." It's my sister Mary. Big Bossy, I call her. "Get out of the way," she orders as she pulls out her coat.

"I ain't goin'." I step out from between my da's uniform

and my ma's fur. Out from the warm closet and into the chilly front room.

"William Jarlath McDermott, for the love of God, you best get your church clothes on and help your sisters with their coats." My ma marches past me and down the hall. When Ma means business, she uses my christened name. And she means business right now.

The thing is, what good did church do for my da? And all that praying we did for him? He's still sitting in that hospital, and he don't remember who he is. Shell shock, they call it. Almost a year and all those candles Ma lights ain't done him no good.

"Can we go see Da at the hospital?" my sister, Anna, asks while I button her coat.

Ma bustles into the room. "Not today. Tie those shoes up." We used to visit Da every Sunday, but during the two months after Christmas we've slacked off. The walk is cold and the trolley costs money.

Da doesn't know us anymore. But the doctor says his memory might improve with time. I sure hope it does. He should know I ain't a little shaver anymore. He should know I'm the man of the house now.

Sometimes I think he's faking it. Just being lazy so he don't have to go back to work. So he don't have to come home with the blood under his fingernails. The blood from the butchering they done at the packinghouse.

The worst part of me wishes he'd died in the war and been a hero. I'm ashamed about that part. Timmy never says it, but I know what people think. Shell shock means my da is yellow, not man enough to be strong and fight the war memories. Not man enough like Timmy's da, who come back from the war more fighting mean than when he left. Not man enough to work so his wife can raise the family. Not man enough to be looking for a job, even.

When I grow up, I'll be man enough to be a soldier that don't get shell shock. I'll save my unit, maybe my whole company, and still come back to take care of my family.

On the way to church we walk past a group of high school boys, hanging around on the street. People call them the Hamburgs. They're all joined up in an athletic club.

One of them tips his cap to me. It's Mickey. I seen him before.

"Don't you be thinking the likes of them is something, Billy," my ma hisses and shoos us along faster. "They're trouble. You stay away."

Da never had no good words for them Hamburgs, neither. "Too big for their britches," he used to say. "Looking for trouble."

But I don't know. Last time Ma sent me to the meat market, Mr. O'Doulle only give me two puny slices for my pennies. Mickey grabbed my arm on the way out the store and stuck a foot-long, four-inch-round beef stick into the crook of my elbow. Then he run off with his gang.

'Course, I never told Ma where the meat come from. They prolly pinched it, what with me busy at the counter with Mr. O'Doulle. I wasn't born yesterday. But still, it was grand they give it to me, wasn't it? They sure ain't no cowards, those Hamburgs.

We round the corner and I see our parish, Nativity of Our Lord, right across from where Ma gets her spices and stamps. I look up and up and up, just like always, until I see the tiny windows in the little dome under the cross. Someday I aim to find the stairs to those windows and have me a look-see.

Mary gives my back a shove and we all troop up the steps. Timmy waits for me in the back of the church.

"Is it okay, Ma?" I ask.

She nods and pushes my sisters ahead of her to the front. She keeps flipping her head round to see we don't sit in the last row. 'Course, we don't want to sit in that row, anyway. We got to be closer to the front to heckle our friends, Connor and Kevin, the altar boys for today.

"Did your da find a job?" I whisper.

"Maybe. He still don't know. My da says it's them blacks. Scabs, he calls them." He spits in his fist and wipes it on my pants.

I clean off my pants with the sleeve of my jacket. "Whaddya mean scabs? Like a sore?"

"No, dummy. Are you just off the boat? They don't join the unions so they can work cheap."

"What's wrong with that? I'd rather work than strike." I heard about strikers. They stand outside and yell stuff. Seems ungrateful to me—at least they have a job.

"Don't you get it?" Timmy's voice is getting loud as we slide into the front row. "The strikers are trying to teach the owners a lesson. Pay them fair and square and treat them right, or they aren't going to work. And then those blacks just march right in and do the job for less money." He knocks my cap off.

I give him a kick on the back part of his leg. "So, where's your da going to work then?"

"Stock Yard, maybe. Finds out tomorrow. Nothin' at the mill or the railroad that ain't been taken by those scabs. But the Stock Yard manager says he don't want no dirty hands touching the livestock."

"Why don't they wash their hands?"

Timmy laughs out loud and slaps my knee. "That's a good one, Billy."

I want to tell him I ain't being funny, but a lady frowns at us and puts her finger to her lips.

Just then, Connor and Kevin come from the side hall, walking with their eyes straight ahead, serious-like, carrying the incense holder and the incense. Timmy gives out a hearty cough.

"Start sneezing," he whispers.

Between the two of us, we sound worse than last year's epidemic. And it works. Connor starts to giggle and Kevin jerks the incense holder. The noise coming out of Timmy sounds for all the world like the whooping cough. I sneeze and laugh at the same time and a snort comes out.

I look up and see Ma, her face mashed up tighter than a cabbage, shooting daggers from her eyes. Holy Mother of God, she's madder than a wet hen. Just then a handbag bonks first me, then Timmy on the head.

"Ow!" yells Timmy.

"Gol dang," I whisper, and we sink down in our seats and shut up just as Father Flaherty makes the sign of the cross.

"In the name of the Father, the Son, and the Holy Ghost," he says.

"The three in one," whispers Timmy. "Me, myself, and I."

He always says that, every time. It's his joke. I nudge him and nod.

When Mass is over, we file out of the church, hoping our folks hurry. We wait on the landing just before the stairs to go out, and the reflection from the stained glass manger scene at the back of the sanctuary makes us glow like the saints we ain't.

Right here, on this very spot, there used to be a livery stable, and don't you know our dear Lord was born in a stable? We learned all about it in church school class. So they named the parish Nativity of Our Lord. That's brilliant, ain't it? I think about that stable a lot in the summer, when the stink of the stockyards knocks me over and I wonder if our dear Lord ever got used to the smell of livestock.

The stairs of Nativity of Our Lord go straight up right as you enter to keep the dirt and stink out of the church. Once you leave the landing you've got no choice but to go down and out. Which is grand if you want to rush off and play a game of stickball, but not so grand if your folks dillydally and you end up standing around with the cold seeping into your blood.

Timmy's da looks grizzled, like he needs a good shave and a douse of cold water.

"Good day, Mr. Beatty."

"Good day, yourself," he says, and he hits my shoulder. "You boys staying out of trouble?"

"Yes sir," I say.

He turns toward Timmy. "Not what your ma says. Come along, boy." And he takes Timmy by the neck and walks away. Timmy looks back at me and pretends he's hitting a ball, so I know he'll be by later for a game.

I think about my da. How he never called me boy. How most Sundays he give us all a peppermint stick if we were good in church. It's weird, the things I remember. Getting a whack on the mouth for sassing Ma and using a bad word. Screaming our fool heads off in the bleachers when Joe Jackson let one fly over the wall. Da wiping his eyes, holding little Anna on the day she joined the world.

Anna's all growed up now. Four years old. Da never did see Ma's last baby, wee little Brian. Born and died. Gone to be with our dear Lord, just like that. Full of the fever and the cough, catching the epidemic in the hospital. The grippe, they called it, and when wee Brian was born, Ma says the hospital was near to overflowing with cases.

And now Joe Jackson is a lousy American for not joining up to go to war. Least that's what the papers say. I don't know. Ma don't never take me to see the White Sox, even though I help out and don't say bad words—leastways not when she can hear—so I ain't seen Shoeless Joe myself in ages. I'd like to ask my da about it. Man to man. Do people have to join up and go to war to be a hero?

Ma and Mary come down the steps, swinging Anna between them, and we head for home. The icy north wind is at our backs all the way, barreling over the frozen edges of Lake Michigan. But it's the end of February and that's a relief. When we get home, I run all the way up the three flights of stairs to our apartment and crash straight into Mr. Weinstein, our skinny boarder.

"Where's the fire?" he says, but he can't say his w sound, so it comes out, "Vere's zee fire?"

Mr. Weinstein always tells us he works for the railroad, but when I shine shoes at the depot I ain't never seen him. Me and Big Bossy think he's strange and suspicious and pretend he's a Russian or German spy. A Bolshevik, which I think is a fancy word for a communist.

He stays in my old room, so I sleep with Mary and Anna. We're making do, Ma says, on account of my da being in the hospital and all. Seems like I'm the one making do, but I don't complain.

"Will you tell your mother I won't be staying for the Sunday meal?" Mr. Weinstein adjusts his thick glasses and covers his huge Adam's apple with his scarf. Mary and I like to make fun of Mr. Weinstein, and I'm pretty good at mocking his accent. I plan on telling Ma, "I vill not be eating viz you," in Mr. Weinstein's stuck-up voice.

I watch him tuck a small box into his overcoat pocket as he turns toward the door. Contraband, I bet. Ammunition. He's up to no good, and I got my eye on him.

I got sums to finish up, and penmanship for school. Pages and pages, so I quick get started so I don't have to help out with Sunday dinner. Ma fusses if our homework ain't done before we skip out on Sundays.

Timmy yells for me from the street as I wolf down my last two bites of dinner. Before Ma can say "fiddlesticks," I jump up, grab my mitt and my marbles, and hurtle down the stairs two at a time.

Me and Timmy been friends long as I can remember. Prolly on account of his ma and my ma being friends long as I can remember, too. We all spent lots of time together while our das were gone to war.

Things are different now that the war is over. Mrs. Beatty don't ever stop by. I heard Ma tell Mrs. O'Connor that Mr. Beatty thinks he can rule the roost with nothing but a cock-a-doodle-doo. And that sounds about right, from the looks of it.

"Did you finish your homework?" I ask Timmy.

"Nah. My da don't care about that sissy stuff. He's teaching me to fight. Says I got to stand up for myself, with the town getting overrun with Southerners."

"Really? Think he'd teach me some, too?" My da don't believe in knocking people around. But he ain't here.

"If he don't get a job, he might. You gotta move your feet, quick, like this." And Timmy dances around me, jabbing me with his fists. "Or you'll get clocked." He pulls back his hair and I see his ear is swollen and bloody inside.

Gol dang. Timmy sure is hard-boiled. I need to toughen up. Maybe him and me ought to join up to be soldiers together.

We run down to our usual spot in the alley off Halsted, where the empty factory sits, and take turns hitting balls to each other. I field better than Timmy, but it don't matter he can't catch, cause the factory fence makes a great backstop.

"Come on," Timmy says after a while. "Let's check the burn pile."

We squeeze under the fence and run behind the factory. Somebody bought the old building, and they're fixing it up, leaving rubbish in the burn pile as they clean the place out. Last time we were here, we uncovered a couple of skinny wooden drawers and used them to make blocks for a snow house.

"Gol dang, would you look at that?" I yell. A flat tray, big as a table, teeters on the edge of the pile. Poking out from each corner are coaster wheels, each bigger than a roller skate's.

"What's it for?" Timmy asks as we grapple with it.

"Don't know. Maybe it's a trolley for loading stuff, or one of them creepers for sliding under a machine."

The corner is bent up, so when we plop it upright there's still one wheel that can't touch the ground. Timmy stands on the edge and I try to keep it level, but it's no use.

Timmy jumps off. "I got an idea. Tip it over."

We hoist it back over and Timmy shows me where to stand. Then he takes a flying leap and lands right beside me on the bent-up corner. *Blam*. And it's fixed.

We ride that trolley up and down our neighborhood, all afternoon, until dark slides up on us. We sled, with no snow, down streets with inclines. The best ride comes when Timmy runs along pushing the cart, then jumps on next to me. We hoot and holler, and crash every time, since we can't steer it. We talk about how next time we'll invent a steering apparatus. Then we stash our flatbed roller coaster car at Timmy's, since he has a yard, and I walk home.

Ma has her feet up when I saunter through the door, pleased as punch with my Sunday afternoon. Me and Timmy always have fun. Ma works hard during the week, taking in piecework from the dress shop and working the breakfast shift at the diner. She gets two dollars a day, when the tips are good and the piecework is steady. Half, she says, of what my da used to get for packing the meat. But she always says, what's done is done and the good Lord will see fit to bless us in due time.

And while she's waiting for that blessing, it's my job to be the man of the family. Timmy's da finds out tomorrow about that Stock Yard job, so tomorrow I aim to march right up and ask if he'll take me on to be his errand boy. I'm strong, for the size of me, and I ain't afraid of cows. And I will make right sure my hands are clean when Mr. Beatty takes a look at me.

Chapter Two

I'M BONE-TIRED AND THAT'S THE truth. But I sit up right quick when Sister Salmonetti raps me on the head.

"Billy McDermott, stand up. What are the inalienable rights granted by the Bill of Rights?"

My brain jogs in place for a few seconds while I scramble around in my head. "The right to bear arms. The right to assemble. The right to . . ."

I fumble for the rest. Somebody giggles.

Sister Salmonetti taps my desk. "Fifty times. After school."

I want to grab her black habit and yank it off. Instead,

the horrid guilt for my rash thoughts plunges me down into my seat, red-faced and sorry. Ma says I get ugly when I'm tired.

And I'm tired because of the work after school. Not the easy work of opening and closing stockyard gates and running orders. Timmy's da didn't get the job at The Union Stock Yard. And after, Timmy said he went on a drinking bender for two weeks. It got so bad, Mrs. Beatty packed Timmy and the baby off to her mother's. But when Mr. Beatty dried out, they moved back and Timmy came by to tell me his da got a job unloading barges on the South Branch of the Chicago River, with Timmy helping out after school. He might have a job for me, he said. The next week at Mass, Timmy's da jabbed the muscles in my arm and told me to show up at the docks on Monday.

And that's how come for three days me and Timmy been running the loads up to the flatbeds. Try as I might, I can't pry my eyelids open long enough to get through my schoolwork. Ma's been out these last two nights working the supper shift so she don't know I'm dragging my tail in when Mary's dishing up the potato stew. And she's none the wiser.

At the end of the school day, Sister Salmonetti sits, watching me work like the devil finishing sentences: I

WILL LEARN MY LESSONS. I WILL LEARN MY LESSONS. I'm nearing the end of the last chalkboard, the chalk just a nub between my fingers, when she stands up and walks toward me. She slaps an envelope down on the chalk ledge. Give this to your mother," she says. Then she turns and leaves, her black robe swishing out behind her.

I stuff the letter in my shirt pocket and run out the door, fast, like trouble is biting at my heels. *I will learn my lessons,* I tell myself. *I will. And make my ma proud.*

Mary is waiting for me, on account of I couldn't tell her to go on ahead. Timmy's prolly at the river already, but it's raining, so I don't know for sure.

"Keep out of the puddles, Billy," says Big Bossy.

"Shut up." I step hard and the splash hits her coat.

"You big goop, you!" She starts to run and I follow, the envelope poking me in the chest, reminding me what a disappointment I am.

Ma opens the envelope when she gets home, her bottom lip getting fat and wiggly. She swipes at her eyes with her sweater sleeve.

"I'm sorry, Ma. I shoulda done better."

Ma looks at me long and sad. "Ah, Billy. It's not you. Sister says we're too far behind in the tuition payments, God help us. I expect they'll be dropping you and Mary."

17

Mary lets out a shriek. "But I'm top of the class. And my friends! It's not my fault Billy gets in trouble. That's why they don't want us."

"Is not, wisenheimer. I get good marks." Next time I'll make sure Mary falls in the puddle, right on her big you-know-what. Then a jolt of an idea hits me. "Can't Mary stay in school? I can drop out and get a job."

"Jaysus, Mary, and the wee donkey, Billy. You're eleven. What job will you get?"

Mary pipes up, "I watch over the Dolans' wee ones most Saturdays and I don't make peanuts."

I think hard. *There's free schools, ain't there?* The answer comes to me and I snap my fingers. "What about public? I can go to public. It'll save money."

Ma puts her hand around my chin. "So like your da, thinkin' of others first. Maybe they will consider keeping Mary, if you can go to public for a year or two. But mind you, just until we get back on our feet. And your da . . ." But her voice catches.

Mary rushes to hug her and Ma pulls both of us in. "I'm real sorry, Billy. Lord have mercy."

I pretend it's a blow, sacrificing for my family. But really, I feel lucky. No more Sister Salmonetti's ruler rapping my knuckles, reminding me that the Dear Lord is mighty disappointed in my behavior and my studies. And no more walking in Mary's footsteps. Maybe little Anna will make a better go of it, or maybe Mary's footsteps won't be so deep with expectations by the time Anna's ready for school. And maybe I can be the top of the class in public school, where the work ain't so hard. I hear tell there's a rough lot there, but I ain't scared. My da didn't raise no coward.

When the rain stops I wander on over to Timmy's house. Mrs. Beatty answers the door with a rag over her nose and cheek. "Such a cold I've got," she says, when she sees me staring. "Let me call for Timmy." She leaves the door open, but don't invite me in.

And she don't sound like she's got a cold when she hollers for Timmy. I see there's a chair upended, and the baby's crying. I hear a door slam and a shadow passes by the back window, heading down the alley, and it sure looks like Mr. Beatty. I stay standing out on the porch and after quite a while Timmy slides out the door and shuts it. His eyes are rubbed red and his nose is dripping. He wipes it on his sleeve, then sits down slow, like an old man.

"No work today?" I say, sitting down next to him. Not knowing what else to say.

"Nah. Too rainy. Ma sent me to Schaller's Pump to find Da, 'cause she needed milk for the baby."

And it don't take adding two plus two to know how that turned out, what with the rag on his ma's cheek and Timmy sitting so carefully.

"I just come by to tell you I'm quitting Nativity. Going to James Ward next week."

"What for?"

"It's the money. But I ain't sad about it. I heard tell there's not so much homework."

"That's where they send the delinquents—remember Frankie? But you don't got to worry. I'll let Mickey know. He'll keep an eye out for you." Timmy slaps my leg. "Hey, you should go out with a bang at Nativity. Let's make a plan."

So until it's time for me to get home for supper that's what we do. Timmy tells me a couple of stories from the ones his da tells him about William Horace de Vere Cole, the biggest Irish prankster working in London's Parliament.

"One time Mr. Horace de Vere Cole brought loads of horse manure in his suitcase on his honeymoon boat trip to San Marco Island. When nobody was looking he dropped the manure all over the plaza and everybody went crazy looking for the horse since no horses live on San Marco," Timmy says. "Ain't that something?"

"But on his honeymoon? Whaddya think his wife had to say about that?"

"She probably thought it was a dirty trick," he says, and we almost fall off the steps laughing.

"Another time Horace got the seating chart to the theater and figured out which seats would spell out a not-nice word. Then he bought tickets for those seats and gave them away just to bald men." Timmy takes off my cap and rubs my hair. "You know how shiny bald heads are. Well, when the bald men sat down everybody in the balcony could see the bald heads shining under the lights, and the bad word was spelled right out."

"What word?" I ask.

"I don't know. Whaddya think?" We puzzle about that for a bit, whispering all the bad words we know.

But in the end, we decide those pranks ain't practical for us, on account of we don't know very many bald men, and bringing horse turds to school might be too tricky. But I know Timmy's got something up his sleeve.

And sure enough, while I'm cleaning out my desk at the end of the next day I hear a commotion. Our friends Kevin and Connor are pointing to the rubbish bin where I been throwing my balled-up, unfinished assignments.

"Snake," Florence screams and jumps out of her seat. Every girl and a few boys streak toward the front of the class, and Sister Salmonetti jumps up on her chair as quick as lightning. In the hubbub Timmy puts some white powder in the middle of our reader and sneaks around behind Miss Salmonetti's desk, slams the book shut hard and the white powder clouds up into the air. Everyone up in the front starts sneezing so hard and so many times that they look like they're catching the grippe.

Before anybody can figure out what's happened, Timmy slips the black snake—the snake that weren't nothing but a piece of garden hose—into his shirt and stacks up his homework, looking as innocent as a baby. It's me that can't stop laughing, and when Sister Salmonetti rings the bell she gives me such an evil eye, I'm worried about my soul.

On our way to the docks we pretend to sneeze and scream, then double over laughing, and do it all over again.

"Where'd you get that sneezing powder?"

"Mickey pinched it for me from his da's friend. Cachoo, it's called. I've a mind to put a little bit in my da's newspaper, the bloody no-good sap. Whaddya think?" Timmy's still sore about the beating his da give him, and I know he's been hanging around Schaller's waiting for his da. But still, his tough talk surprises me. He shows me what's left of the powder, folded up tight in a little packet.

"I wouldn't, if I was you."

"Yeah? Well, Mickey saw what happened to me at Schaller's, and he says he won't stand for it if my da ever lays a hand on me again."

I nod. That Mickey is all right. And I'm glad he's looking out for Timmy since I won't be with him at Nativity anymore. "I'll still see you every day at the docks," I tell him as we come up to Archer Avenue.

So here I am, Monday morning, standing outside the doors of James Ward School, a massive, three-story school made of red-brown brick, except for the limestone eyebrows on the windows and the stripes around its belly. I heard tell the toilets are in the basement, which is a bonus, since some other public schools still have privies out in the schoolyard.

On Saturday, the day after I told Timmy I was going to James Ward, a couple of the Hamburg boys stopped me on the sidewalk. They told me not to worry. Mickey wanted me to know they'd be watching out for me. Imagine that. It made me feel important. But in bed that night, I got to thinking. Who's doing the watching? What are they watching out for? And then it felt like they might be spying on me, trying to see if I was brave enough to be a Hamburg. Brave enough to be trusted.

I'm standing here, wondering about it, with a swarm of kids rushing by me as if the devil himself is on their heels. At Nativity, the sisters opened the carved doors every morning and we solemnly paraded in. Here, I'm swept along into the hall. I'm heading to Room 204 and I figure it will be upstairs. Right away, I notice all the walls are brick with no stained glass. And suddenly I miss the order and the holiness of Nativity.

I stand in the door of Room 204, not sure what to do, until the teacher motions me to her desk. Her dark hair is piled up on her head and her green eyes sparkle at me, and I feel loads less nervous. I see she holds my report card in her hand.

"Welcome, William. I'm Miss Benson. What brings you here from Nativity? You've decent marks I see." She's not old. Not like the sisters.

When I don't answer she shrugs and shakes her head. She prolly thinks I'm like Frankie who got kicked out of Nativity for calling Sister Catherine a you-know-what when she rapped his knuckles.

"Put your supplies here." She motions to a seat and says,

to a boy in the seat behind mine, "Foster, see to it that William gets his books from the shelf."

I follow Foster to the bookshelf. Rays of dusty light shine from the three windows over the bookshelf and I figure that way is east. And if that's east, then the two windows on the other wall must be facing south. South toward Wentworth and the black neighborhoods.

James Ward sits on the edge of my Irish neighborhood, but I never really thought about going to school with kids from other neighborhoods. At Nativity everyone was all white and all Irish, except Frankie, who's part Italian. And going to public school, too, now.

It's not hard to see Foster is a black boy. I never talked to anyone black before, except at Anderson's Fish Shop. Oh, and one of the Pullman porters at Central Station.

"How's business?" the porter always asks me when I'm there shining shoes.

"It'd be better if you sit down," I say every time. And every time he laughs.

I don't believe I ever had cause to talk to a black boy before in my life. But I aim to start now. "I'm Billy," I say.

But Foster doesn't say anything to me, just piles up books in my arms, keeping his eyes on my feet. His hands are the color of my baseball glove and his fingernails are ragged and chewed.

"You live around here?" I try again.

"My auntie do." Foster's voice is low and slow. "You?" When he lifts his eyes to my face I see they are the darkest dark brown I ever saw.

"I got kicked out of Nativity of Our Lord."

He steps away from me. "I don't want no trouble." And his eyes get big in his round face.

"Not for being bad. For not having money."

"Well, that ain't no crime. Ain't nobody got money." And he laughs and points at his shoes with holes all through them. They're the same as my shoes, scuffed with no hope left, and we both wear shabby wool jackets over our overalls. A pin holds the bottom of his closed on account of a missing button.

I look around the room, to see the way things are. The girls outnumber the boys. I see three more black boys besides Foster, four boys that look a little like Frankie, and about five that look like me. I walk past a girl with blond pigtails and accidentally bump her elbow.

"Beg pardon," I say.

"Eat ees an order," she says, with the same sort of accent as Mr. Weinstein's.

Foster whispers, "That's Anika. She can't talk English."

I guess it's a regular kaleidoscope in public school. And Foster's right; nobody here has very much. Everybody looks a bit tattered, not tucked and polished like at Nativity.

After only an hour or so I already can tell who's the class clown and who's the most popular girl, and when the morning is about done I know I'm behind in math and ahead in English.

Miss Benson runs a tight ship. Not as tight as Sister Salmonetti, but still, by noon, I'm happy for lunch and I head home lickety-split and charge through the door.

"Ma? Ma?" I call as I wander through the front room and into the kitchen. I'm a little disappointed no one's home for lunch. I wolf down the cheese sandwich Ma set out on the table for me, feeling a mite sorry for myself. Having to come home for lunch sure cuts into my recess options. At Nativity we got hot lunch, served up by the nuns. I pat the pocket that I always keep my ringer and my cat eyes in. I got nobody to talk to and nothin' to do and more than half my lunch hour left.

I take a zigzag path back to school, cutting through alleys and angling up toward James Ward. That's when I see Foster and his friends. They're playing stickball in an empty lot a couple of blocks from school. Foster whacks at a wad of rags with a plank of wood and takes off running for first base. I watch for a couple of minutes, missing the lads from Nativity, wondering how they're getting on without me. Wondering who's winning Ante Over, and who lost their ringer in marbles today. Then I trudge back to James Ward.

I'm hardly prepared when Miss Benson dismisses us at the end of the day, so accustomed to the extra hour of school at Nativity, but I ain't heartbroken. No sirree. I jolt out of my seat, light as a feather with hardly any books to carry home for homework, and head toward my house to grab my jacket before heading to the docks, on account of the day's turned cloudy and gray. Most everybody heads for the neighborhoods to the west as they leave the school building.

From the side of my eye I see Foster and his friends on the corner opposite mine, about to cross the street and go the same way as me. I'm puzzled 'cause I thought they'd live the other way, where all the black folks live. I stop walking to let them catch up, but a big, bristly-haired boy keeps pushing Foster and his friends back every time they try to cross. Foster takes something from his lunch satchel and puts it in the boy's hands. Then he and his friends run. When they're just about even with me, his friends turn around and head back the way they come, but Foster keeps walking.

"Hey," I yell over to him and he stops walking and faces me.

"Hey, yourself," he yells back.

"What happened to your friends?"

"They was just helping me cross the street."

"What did that boy want?"

"His sandwich."

"Why you got his sandwich?"

He shrugs and tilts his head to the side like I should be able to figure it out.

"Do you got his sandwich every day?" I ask.

"Only on the days when I want to walk down this here street," he says. And he turns away from me. I watch him half run, half walk until he gets to the corner and turns down Twenty-Ninth Street. I keep walking, a little drizzle spitting on me, until I get to Thirty-First, still trying to puzzle out what I saw. Why didn't the boy want Foster to walk this way? What if Foster didn't give him a sandwich? Does Foster have two sandwiches, or did he save his lunch to give away?

After I leave my house, I wait for Timmy near Nativity. I'm busting to tell him all about James Ward. Who knows?

Maybe his da might let him switch schools when he finds out it's not so bad, and it costs nothing. I bend down to tie my ever-loving frizzled shoelace for the hundredth time and a second later I feel two hands over my eyes.

"Guess who?" Timmy's voice says.

I stand and sock him a good one, and then we race each other up Thirty-Fifth Street. It's raining good now, and we stop to catch our breath under an awning painted with big white words: BENTON HOUSE OF HAPPINESS.

"So, how was it?" Timmy asks.

"Good. A regular fruit basket of kids."

"Yah? Like what?" But he doesn't wait for me to answer. Instead he scoots in the door of the Benton House just as a mother comes out of it with her little one.

"What're you doing?" I whisper, following him in. He leads us toward a room at the end of the hall. Babies fuss and little shavers dart about while a lady in a white apron goes back and forth from the room, delivering something on a tray to the other rooms. She gives us the once-over, but Timmy keeps his head up and his walk direct. We pass a big room, full of windows, where kids about our age are keeping busy, the girls sewing and the boys sanding wood. Timmy waits until the lady in the apron comes out of the room with another tray, and then he pulls me in.

I gasp. More cookies than I ever seen fill plates next to little metal cups of milk on a long table, like the table in the painting of the Last Supper hanging on the wall at Nativity.

"Shh," says Timmy and drains first one, then another of the cups. He crams one cookie into his mouth whole, stuffing most the rest from the plate into his pocket. I'm slow to catch on, but manage to slurp some milk and grab a handful of the remaining cookies before the door opens.

"What in the Sam Hill is going on?" the lady in the apron says, but we don't hear more—we're already running for the exit. Just before we bust out into the rain, Timmy takes an umbrella from the brass stand by the door, and when we get far enough away, we stop and stand under it, eating our cookies.

"Ain't that stealing?" I ask.

"Nah, I'll put it back tomorrow."

"I mean the cookies," I say, spraying crumbs from my mouth as I talk.

"Ma worked there a couple of times, as a substitute when somebody took sick. She ain't got paid yet, so I figure we got an advance coming."

"Your mom works there?" I ask.

"She would if my da'd let her. She's got some schooling,

you know. Benton's a day school for wee ones to stay in while their folks work at the stockyard offices or the factories."

That gives me a thought. Maybe Ma can bring Anna there. She'd love it. "Is it free?"

"Are you off with the fairies? 'Course not. Only thing free is the charity they give out to all those black Southerners coming up here, sponging off those of us who don't got a pot to pee in." Timmy digs in his pockets for more cookies.

"Some of those Southerners work, don't they? At the stockyards and the factories?" I'm thinking of how Timmy's da said he lost his job at the steel mill to those Southerners. So they can't all be living off charity. But I shouldn't have said it, because it just riles Timmy up.

"Sure. Taking jobs away from us. Just like your Russian spy, living in your house, taking charity from your ma, stealing a good job at the railroad—a job my da could of got." He collapses the umbrella and starts walking. The rain is just a drizzle again.

I hold my tongue, but what he said ain't true. Mr. Beatty ain't got enough book learning to work at the railroad office like Mr. Weinstein, and anyway with my da in the hospital, Ma needs the money Mr. Weinstein pays us. And the wee ones in Benton House of Happiness seemed to be doing okay, chubby cheeked and dressed properly.

Not like the kids at James Ward. What's wrong with charity if somebody needs it? I think again about Foster and the sandwich and wish I could share my cookies with him.

Chapter Three

THE NEXT DAY MISS BENSON starts out with a history lesson. I only half-listen because we done studied Abraham Lincoln at Nativity on his birthday in February. Then she makes a list on the chalkboard: THE CIVIL WAR. ABRAHAM LINCOLN. 1863. THE EMANCIPATION PROCLAMATION. "Write an essay on how the Civil War changed the United States," she says.

I think about my da and the song he used to sing about his kin fighting the war in Ireland. The Easter Rising, they called it, and Ma says it's not over yet. I guess it's more like our Revolutionary War, here, when the colonies wanted to be independent from Great Britain, but it's also like the Civil War because the Irish are all fighting against each other, too. Not everybody agrees with the plan to split from Great Britain.

I hum a little bit of the tune my da used to sing when he was shaving, about the green flag and the crown rag, and I get a little knot in my throat thinking about wars.

Then Miss Benson asks everybody to think about a time when they experienced a violation of someone's inalienable rights to inspire us when we write our essay. And I'm right glad I learned all about those inalienable rights from Sister Salmonetti.

I remember one time when I was little we went to see the State Street parade. A mean white man pushed a black man down on the sidewalk and my da yelled at him to stop. The white man just turned around and punched my da. I remember Ma yelling at Da: "For the love of God, quit minding other people's business."

Afterward, my da gathered Ma and me and the girls all around him, his eye swelling shut, and he said, "Mind me now. The great Mr. Lincoln lived and died by the idea that 'all men are created equal.' I aim to abide by that. Some people think there's a line, and if everybody stays on their side of the line, then we'll all get along just fine." My da drew a line in the air and put his two hands on each side of it. Big, strong hands, from lifting meat all day. "But sometimes to stand up for what's right you have to cross the line. Only a coward don't stand for what he believes. I ain't no coward and none of you best be one either."

I think about that now. About my da and what he believes. And I think about the two wars, the Civil War and the Great War. The Civil War took away slavery and unfairness, but it also took away lots of lives and homes. Over 600,000 soldiers died, Miss Benson says, not counting the ones who got diseases. And the president got shot.

The Great War took away lots of lives, too. Millions, they say. And my da, my bedroom, and my school. Thinking about everything that war takes away, I bend over my paper and start writing.

Why do we have wars? To keep us free.

I stop writing and do some more thinking. Free from what? I ask myself. The newspaper says it's to be free from the Central Powers. I'm a little fuzzy on it. But I think the Central Powers want to take over everything, and the United States and the other good countries worked together to take away their power.

Do wars really make us free? It sure don't seem like

Foster and his friends are free to do everything. He can't even cross the road without giving up his sandwich. And my ma ain't free from the worries the war brought on our family. Even I ain't free to do as I like.

I get back to writing, trying to make sense of my thoughts.

When it's lunchtime Miss Benson says we'll work on the essays in the afternoon and maybe read a few out loud when we finish them. We all skedaddle out the door. The outside smells are starting to wake up from their winter naps. Some of them fresh, like wood and grass, and some of them are foul, like spoilt milk and horse turds. I run home, eat the lunch Ma made, and reread my *Boy's Life* magazine. And I'll be doggoned if page three don't make me wish for summer:

> *We know a chap gets a longing just about now to be out-of-doors. Snow is melting and brooks are springing to life. Suckers are beginning to stir themselves, robins are here, and the wren's song ripples under your window like a silvery alarm clock. Sure, you get spring fever. Most of us do, and it just seems as if we can't wait until we've finished our work.*

I head back to school, going the same zigzag way past the empty lot. I glance sideways at Foster and his friends, who are back at it again, hitting that rag ball with their stick. And I suddenly get an idea for tomorrow. There ain't no harm in asking if I can play, is there?

So the very next day, after arithmetic, grammar, and some more work on our essays, I hightail it home and wolf down the potato Ma wrapped up in a hot towel before she left and the end of a sausage stick.

Then I stuff my baseball in my pocket and reach under the corner of my mattress for my glove. It's my da's lucky glove that he caught a foul ball in from Buck Weaver, who plays third base for the White Sox. I never let nobody touch it, not even Timmy, and I keep it hidden. Having a little sister like Anna makes me skittish about leaving my important stuff out in the open. Wouldn't take a second before she'd be using my glove as a bed for her dolly.

I run out of the house, zigzag through the streets, and walk right up to the edge of the empty lot.

"Hey! Hey, Foster." They all stop, eyeing me like I'm the boogeyman. I pull my baseball from my pocket. "Come on. Let's play."

Nobody says anything for a whole minute, and I start

to worry they don't want me, when finally Foster nods his head and motions me over.

"Y'all know Billy?" he says.

We have a great game. With five of us we can field the ball so it never gets out of the lot. I'm the only one with a glove. Foster is a powerful hitter, and the others ain't bad either. Not to be mean, but they're much better than Timmy. By the time lunch is over, my school pants have a hole in the knee, and I got four new friends. Foster and me talk about baseball the whole way back to the school.

"Ever been to a game?" I ask.

Foster shakes his head. "Nah. But I got some baseball cards."

"Who you got that's good?"

"Joe Jackson."

"Really? Boy, I'd like to see that. He's one of my favorites."

"You can have it. I'm a Browns fan. Got any Browns?"

I'm stupefied. "A Browns fan?"

"My Daddy is a Browns fan. I guess 'cause we come from Jackson, Mississippi. The St. Louis Browns is closer to us."

"Well, that don't mean you can't be a White Sox fan."

"Okay." Foster nods and puts out his hand. "I'm a White Sox fan."

I shake his hand, pretty proud of myself for converting a Browns fan. *Maybe I'll be a salesman when I grow up,* I think.

Miss Benson gives us disapproving looks as we rush to our seats late, after the class is all settled down.

While everybody is doing their sums, Miss Benson calls me over and opens a reader in front of her.

"William," she says. "Please read out loud, starting here." And she opens to page 105, "The Seven Sticks."

I do my best to impress her with my vocabulary and inflections just the way Sister Salmonetti expected us to read our lessons.

"All right, William. Thank you. What is the lesson of the Seven Sticks?"

By golly. I was so busy making an impression I don't remember one thing I read. I keep my eyes down on the reader, ashamed at how stupid I'm getting to be.

"That's all right, William." She smiles at me. "I'm glad to see you're a fine reader. I'm sure your expressive reading distracted your thinking."

And it's the nicest way of telling me I been a fool, so full of myself.

Late in the afternoon, she gets us together in groups of four and five to share the beginnings of our essays. I'm lucky enough to get Foster in my group, along with Helen and Anika. We draw sticks to see who goes first and I pull the short one, so I read my first page.

Helen says, "Miss Benson told us to write how the Civil War changed lives, not the Great War. You didn't follow the directions."

Anika nods and smiles at Helen.

Foster says, "Because of the Civil War my daddy got to fight in the Great War. How's that not following the directions?"

I'm excited hearing his daddy was a soldier like mine. "Where did he fight?"

"France."

"Mine, too," I say, and grin at Foster.

"They was called the Buffalo Soldiers of the Ninety-Second Infantry Division."

"My da was in the 112th Field Artillery."

Helen ahems and starts reading her essay, which is written in such tiny writing that her first page takes three times as long to read as mine did.

Foster fidgets and blinks his eyes, trying not to nod off, and I feel the same.

I don't say nothing, but Helen has stuff in her essay about the women's right to vote, which weren't part of the directions neither.

Then Anika reads her essay: "The Civil War. Abraham Lincoln. 1863. The Emancipation Proclamation."

Foster jabs me with a finger and I cover my mouth just in case a laugh comes busting out. But Helen claps. "Good, very good. If we change the order we can make a sentence." She takes Anika's paper and at the bottom writes, "Abraham Lincoln wrote the Emancipation Proclamation in 1863 after the Civil War."

And then it's time to go home, before Foster can even read his essay.

I run home, change my clothes, and head to the river.

I finally told Ma I got the docker job after a week, when I'd earned enough money to impress her. She worried me something fierce about it. "Billy, don't you get no fancy notions you can run off with the lot of them ruffians. You come straight home afterwards." But I seen the shine in her eye when she put that money in her pocketbook.

Timmy's da tips his hat to me and I get started, loading at least fifty crates and barrels before Timmy even shows up.

Not too long ago they went and built a bridge over the

river. Great for the people who want to get over the bridge. Not so great for the barges that want to go down the river, since the bridge is so low the barges can't fit under it.

So us dockers sort it all, loading it on flatbed wagons or stacking it for pick up. Timmy's da does the heavy unloading and sorting, and we work the pickups, offering to help load the crates and barrels, hoping for tips. The first few days I worked there I was so busy trying to outdo Timmy and prove myself to Timmy's da, while at the same time trying not to get kicked by horses or run over by cars, that I didn't notice too much.

Today my pitching arm is sore, but when there's a lull in the barge traffic I start to pay attention to what's around me. I see some black workers on the barges, sweeping and clearing off the rubbish. There's a kid pulling the broken wooden platform pieces into a pile. It looks like Foster.

I walk down the bank a bit to get closer, and the kid looks at me and puts up his hand. Well, I'll be.

After Timmy shows up, I head back to my usual spot and we work another hour. I like the feel of money in my pockets. If only my da could see me now. He'd be ever so proud, wouldn't he now?

"Where you been?" I ask Timmy when he puts a load on the wagon near me.

"Been running errands for Big Bill and Mickey. Important stuff," he says, sounding full of himself. "How was your school today?"

"Okay. More crowded than Nativity. Not everybody had time to read their essays."

"It's those blacks. Crowding up the city. They should send 'em all back to the South."

"Why?"

"My da says they bring diseases. Mickey says they steal our jobs and trash the city."

"Oh. Well, the ones in my class seem okay."

"You got 'em in your own class?" Timmy aims a wad of spit at my feet.

"So?" I think about playing ball at lunch with Foster and his friends. I think about how Foster is a new White Sox fan, how he's going to give me his Joe Jackson card. I think about how both our dads fought in France. I feel my hand start to make a fist.

But then I think about the plans Timmy and I made for the trolley and how Mr. Beatty's been nice enough to give me a job. I think about how me and Timmy go way back and how he watches out for me. I know about his da's drinking problem and he knows about my da's shell shock.

Timmy says, "Don't forget who got you this job." And he steps toward me.

Before I decide what I'm going to do, Timmy's da walks over and slaps us on our backs. "Ready, Timbo?" He drapes an arm around Timmy's neck, squeezes him tight, and holds out his hand. Timmy fishes in his pockets and hands over his money. When his da lets go, Timmy steps away and folds his arms over his chest, hugging himself. His eyes meet mine, and I know we both wish our das were different. And no lucky penny will make our wishes come true.

"Will you be joining us at Schaller's tonight, Billy?" Mr. Beatty asks me, clomping Timmy hard on the head and pocketing the coins. "Going to raise me a toast to President Wilson putting Negroes in their place in the paper today. 'Being treated as equals in France has gone to their heads,' that's what the president said. Equal to whites—imagine them thinking that. They're nothing but communist scabs, stealing our jobs and ruining our neighborhoods."

Timmy's da knows Ma don't allow me at Schaller's Pump. She didn't even like Da going in there, back before . . . you know.

If Da stopped by the house to change out of his shirt and butchering apron before heading back out, Ma would get all steamed up. "Jaysus give me patience, Mary restrain my tongue. You and the poison. Always tempting you." And she would shake her finger at him. "You be home before that table is set." Well, I bet she wishes he was off at Schaller's now having a pint with Timmy's da, sharing a belly laugh about the Emerald Isle. I get sad right quick when I think about it.

Mr. Beatty and Timmy light out, without a goodbye. I'm still mad at Timmy, but I feel sorry for him too, knowing he will be the one making sure his da gets home in time for supper, his da liking the poison just a little more than everybody else. I feel bad his da treats him rough, especially after a few pints, but his family problems ain't my business, just like my friends ain't Timmy's business.

The weather gets warmer and little green shoots start to poke up out of the dirt, promising to show off their flowers soon. I'm a regular at the empty lot during lunch, and we've got enough players now to make two teams and cover all the bases and the outfield. I find out Foster moved here after his daddy got home from the war, which was a month or two after my da came home and went to the hospital. Maybe they knew each other in France. Maybe they fought together.

Timmy's da fought too, but he fought in the navy,

searching for German submarines that were torpedoing supply ships. Maybe those German torpedoes rubbed off on him, making him meaner than he used to be.

As usual, we cut it close getting back in our seats after our ball game, but Miss Benson has her back turned, putting the reading assignment on the board.

"N—— lover," someone whispers behind me, and I hear a loud thud. I turn in my chair, but everyone is back to working on their essays. Foster's eyes are pinched tight, and he's holding his knee. Somebody must of whacked him something fierce, but he's no tattletale, I see.

We've been working on our essays all week. Copying them over in ink after Miss Benson fixed up all the spelling and grammar and made suggestions for improvement. I made sure to let Helen know that Miss Benson liked my essay just fine.

After I work for a bit, I raise my hand and ask to be excused to visit the water closet, which is what you call a toilet that's not a privy outside.

When I come back, my essay has a big inkblot in the middle and the word N—— LOVER scrawled in the middle.

Gol dang it! I can't even scribble it out, so I have to copy that page over. I stare hard around the room, but I don't see one twitch or smirk. And if Foster ain't going to tattle, neither am I. I wonder if Foster knows who done it. Would he tell me, if he did?

Suddenly a thought occurs to me: *Is this what Mickey means, watching out for me? Is somebody in this class spying on me for Mickey? Watching me play baseball with Foster?* And what's wrong with that, anyway? Ain't we all equal to do what we want to do, just like we're writing about in our essays? Without people being uncivilized and making a mess of our personal property? Jeez Louise! We had the Civil War and now people ain't civil?

But I'm civil, and I don't aim to be a coward. I will join up for that next war and keep us free from those Central Powers. That's one thing my da will be proud of. I send my thoughts out to the heads bent over pens that busily scribble on their essays. *Just call me that horrible name to my face, and we'll see who's the coward.*

After school I check on Ma. She's been poorly for the last couple days so I been watching Anna instead of working at the docks. But it's quiet in the flat. No Anna. No Ma. I change my jacket, slice myself some sponge cake, and pour a glass of milk. I'm just lifting the glass to my lips when a tall, skinny ghost rounds the corner.

I yell out. "Ahhh!" And the glass hits the table, shattering.

An ocean of milk paints the floor and glass sticks up from it like icebergs in the sea.

"Vat are you doing here?" asks Mr. Weinstein.

"What are you doing here?" I ask him back.

"Sick. I verk here today." He points to the kitchen table.

Stacks of receipts and envelopes are dissolving in the splatters of milk on the table, black ink melting into wavy squiggles. And then, just for a second, I see what looks like white powder and tiny wires in the middle of a square of brown paper. But then I blink and Mr. Weinstein is sweeping the wet receipts off the table, trying to save the drier ones underneath, and the powder and wires are gone.

It takes forever to clean up all the glass and milk, and just when I think I'm done, Mr. Weinstein sees another piece of glass. "Ach. Vatch it. Vun more."

By the time I reach the docks, the workers are straggling home and there's only a few wagons left to load. *Darn that Mr. Weinstein. He made me late.* Then I pause, thinking about what I saw. *Is he making bombs for the Bolsheviks? Just like the newspapers are talking about. Or is my imagination getting the better of me?*

I'm just about to give up on earning a few pennies when out of the corner of my eye I see Foster with an armload of broken platforms. He motions to me.

"Wanna see something?" he asks when I walk over.

I follow him behind a fence and down a path that starts up right where the factory property ends and the bridge foundation begins. "Where we going?"

"You gonna see."

Everything around me is still winter gray. Gray branches. Gray sky. Gray dirt. If there's any green starting to sprout up down here, it's hidden in the shadow of the trees. After a bit I see gray water. It's a river, but not the Chicago River. This one is small, more like a creek. It might be part of the canal that goes to The Union Stock Yard. They been talking about cleaning the garbage from the water down along there. I heard tell one time a drunk walked right out on the creek, thinking it was a side-walk. But this here part don't look bad, so maybe we're downstream far enough, or maybe this here's another little feeder stream.

Foster leads me down a steep part of the path to a clearing. Two boys are fishing by the creek, and they turn and see us. A campfire flashes out of the gray. A low tree branch nearby supports a lean-to made out of the wooden platforms from the factories, nailed together, with smaller twigs and logs stuck in between the spaces.

"This is our camp. Me and my brothers'. You like it?"

"Yah. It's grand. What is this place?"

"Bubbly Creek. Hey, Emmett," he calls out. "This here's my friend Billy. Hey, Odell. This is Billy."

I ain't shy, but the cat sure has got ahold of my tongue. I'm full of questions but can't ask them. *Is it okay Foster invited me? Will his brothers be mad? Who else knows about this place? Can you really eat fish out of a creek?*

Emmett, the taller brother, yanks on his line and soon enough a fish dangles out over the water. Emmett is light-skinned, Italian looking. Foster runs over with a crate and Emmett lets the fish flop in. I ain't never been fishing. My da promised to teach me, but he never got the chance.

Foster slices the fish head off and rips out the guts, throwing them back into the river. I'm horrified and amazed at the same time. Then he takes the fish and pokes a pointed stick into the tail and back up near the top. He shifts some of the wood pieces on the fire and crouches down, holding the fish over the coals.

"Are you going to eat that?"

"Sure. Ain't you never ate roasted fish?"

"No. I ain't never fished before."

Foster sings out, "This boy ain't never fished before!"

Emmett and Odell laugh and walk toward the fire. Odell brings another fish and roasts it the same as Foster.

Odell is much darker—darker even than Foster. But when he smiles his teeth shine in the fading daylight.

They offer me some of their fish and we pull flakes of flesh right off the stick. It's good. So good.

The fire is hungry, too. It prowls around the wood pieces, tasting, savoring, devouring, then lifting its flaming tongues toward the sky. My face is warm and I get a little longing for my da to share this feeling of happiness with me. The woods are quiet but for the fire snapping its teeth and licking its lips.

Emmett and Odell tell stories about fishing in Jackson, Mississippi. Roasting corn on the cob and eating until the whites of their eyes turn yellow.

I think it might be the first time I ever had such a wonderful end to my day, and I start to sing, real soft:

Too ra loo ra loo ral. Too ra loo ra lie.
Too ra loo ra loo ral. Hush now, don't you cry.

Pretty soon, Foster picks up the words, and we're both singing.

Too ra loo ra loo ral. Too ra loo ra lie.
Too ra loo ra loo ral. That's an Irish Lullaby.

We sing it one more time, with Odell and Emmett joining in, just as if we're Boy Scouts, out in the wilds on an adventure from my *Boy's Life* magazine.

And then I walk home, the fire smell on my clothes and the song still in my head, thinking about my new friends, and hoping I get invited to come fishing again.

Chapter Four

THIS MORNING'S NEWSPAPER GIVES MY stomach a churn.
Three years ago Murderous Mary, the elephant,
knocked her trainer to the ground with her trunk and
stomped on his head, crushing his skull.

Last night a grizzly bear, Goliath, mauled his dance
partner, swiping her to the ground with his giant bear paw
and sinking his teeth into her neck.

Mary and Goliath are both in the paper today, their
photos right there on the page. One hanging from a crane
and the other splayed out like a rug.

I also read about three black navy sailors who got off

their ship in Charleston, South Carolina, and got killed by four white sailors. Their bodies left hanging from the trees. They call it a lynching. I wonder if they was wearing their uniforms when they got hanged. No wonder Foster's daddy moved them away from the South.

I sure ain't going to be a sailor, like Mr. Beatty and all them navy folks. I might join up in the Field Artillery like my da—redlegs, they call them—'cause of the red stripe down their pants. The Field Artillery blows things up.

There's two more stories about black army veterans getting attacked in Alabama and Georgia. Ain't that something? Up here in the North, when we see soldiers wearing their uniforms we respect them. Seems to me the president should knock some sense into those Southern white folks, but even in Washington, DC things aren't equal. They got separate toilets for blacks and whites, but when someone went to talk to President Wilson about things not being equal he got mad. The newspaper story headline says, WILSON REBUKES NEGRO WHO 'TALKS UP' TO HIM. I wish Teddy Roosevelt hadn't died. He could talk some sense into President Wilson.

Life is unpredictable, I guess. But no. It's more than that for some people, ain't it? It's risky. Like a field of landmines.

My sister Mary comes home from school, eyes red, after kids been heckling her. "They're calling me Murderous Mary," she sobs to Ma.

"It's from the paper," I tell Ma. "The elephant story."

"Ah, Mary. Don't you know, them calling you Murderous Mary is just words. That can't hurt you none." Ma pats Mary's back and looks back at her books.

"Who said it?" I ask. "I'll make them pay."

Mary gulps out a giggle, in between her sobs. "What're you going to do? You're a little pip-squeak."

"Who says?" I punch Mary's arm, not even hard.

"Ow! Ma," she screams.

"Shush, now, the both of you. Can't you see I'm studying?"

Ma wants to be a nurse. There's a shortage, she says. She read it in the newspaper, and one of the workers at my da's hospital, St. Luke's, told Ma about a new program. One year and she can be a practical nurse.

"There's gonna be an entrance exam, don't you know, and I aim to be ready," she says.

I don't tell her it's too late. But it is. Da's empty eyes never change, and wee little Brian, dying over a year and a half ago, don't need a nurse in the ever-after. Ma can't help.

It's up to me now. Up to me to watch over little Anna.

Up to me to stick up for Mary and find out why she sneaks down the stairs at night. Up to me to bring my pennies home to make the short ends meet. And I decide to keep a watchful eye, just like my da would do.

Don't worry, Da. It's a might bit hard, but I ain't no coward.

Oh, and I almost forgot. It's up to me to keep up hope for our White Sox. Opening day is coming right up next week. They're playing the St. Louis Browns. Poor Foster. I wonder if he'll be rooting for the White Sox instead of the Browns. His daddy might call him a turncoat, but I guess there's no better way to prove his new loyalty.

I hope the Sox play better than ever this season. *They might go to the World Series this year, Da,* I think. *They just might.*

It's that watchful eye that gets my suspicions boiling over two nights later. Ma puts Anna to bed and then sits snoring in her chair instead of studying. Mary clears the table and scoots out the door. Mr. Weinstein ain't been home since Sunday dinner. I open the door, quiet-like, and slip out to the stoop. I stand pressed against the wall, my owl eyes adjusting to the dark. This is how God watches the world. High up—knowing who lives where and the secrets of their lives.

Mrs. Ryan lighting a candle for her missing son. Mr. and Mrs. Dunne having their usual row at each other with the screen door open. Patrick Flynn coming to call on his sweetheart Aggie, who used to watch over me and Mary before Anna was born.

And then I see Mary duck behind the stairwell with a fellow. I edge forward as far as I can and see the fellow put his arms around Mary as she lifts her face up and kisses him. Well, I'll be a monkey's uncle.

A big, black car pulls up and the headlights shine right on the fellow's face. I'll be a monkey's uncle two times! It's Joey she's kissing. One of the Hamburgs. Won't Ma have a flying fit when she finds out?

Then I hear a door open and I remember the car. A man gets out of it, then reaches back inside and pulls out a box. A shoebox, maybe. And when he turns I see it's Mr. Weinstein. Mary sees him too, and she runs up our stairs, smacking right into me as she tries to get through the door before Mr. Weinstein starts up the stairs. Neither of us trusts Mr. Weinstein to keep our secrets.

I scurry after her. "Is that your fellow?" I whisper when we're safe in the bedroom, knowing Ma will wake up when she hears Mr. Weinstein let the door bang shut.

"None of your business, nosy," she says.

"Da won't like it," I say, trying to keep my word to Da about watching out for Mary.

"What do you know? He never let me do anything." And Mary flounces down on the bed with the already-sleeping Anna.

It's true, from what I remember. Da was hard on Mary sometimes. Not letting her wear the styles. Not letting her get her hair cut. Not letting her go off with her friends. Expecting her to bring him his tea. He used to tell her, "I got a bit of news for you, Mary. No man fancies a woman who runs around. Now you think about that. Keeping up the house and the cooking. That's what you'll be wanting to learn. There's no more needs to be said, is there?"

I chew on that for a bit, then ask, "Does Ma know?"

"'Course not. She won't let me do anything either. She'd have a fit. You better not tell on me."

"'Course I won't," I say again. But then a little scheming comes into my head. Doing favors for nothing is bad business. "You think one day you can watch Anna for me so I can play baseball? It's so hard to bring her to the field."

"When?"

"I don't know. But I can bring her by the Dolans', if you don't mind."

She looks at me long and hard. "Just once in a while," she answers.

Mary and I both know we just made a deal, but we don't say it. This is how it works. I do a little thing for you and you do a little thing for me. It's the same in politics, isn't it? The election's just around the corner and Mayor Thompson's been making big promises around town. You do this little thing and vote for me and I'll do this little thing and take care of you. Maybe if I do a little thing and find out what Mr. Weinstein is up to, Mayor Thompson'll do a little thing and look out for my family.

It rains a lot now that winter's completely said goodbye and spring's butted on in. On the days when the sun comes out and I'm loading crates and barrels, my back feels warm. It's only April, and I'm already itching for school to be out.

I spend more time with Foster and his brothers than ever I did with Timmy and my old chums. Timmy often skips dock work when he runs errands for Mickey. His da don't mind because there's usually a bottle of liquor or a pint in it for him. That old trolley we stashed in Timmy's yard is prolly all rusted by now from the rain, anyway. Foster and I dragged down more wooden platforms and put an addition on the lean-to, so even when the skies drip their sadness we can all sit inside and watch the river.

I have an awful thirst for fishing, like I been parched my whole life and now I can't get enough to satisfy me. So whenever we can, we do it. Emmett teaches me little tricks.

"Stretch that worm over the hook so the fish can't see the metal."

"Figure out how deep the water is and don't let the hook hit the bottom."

"Don't pull up on the first nibble."

And I get to be almost as good as the three of them.

But whenever we've already caught more than three fish each, Odell always has to remind me, "Ain't no use wasting the bait if there ain't fish in the water."

Emmett has a regular job collecting rubbish with Huizenga's Trash Removal. They pick up from businesses and take the stuff that burns to the reduction plant and the other stuff to the dump on Twenty-Seventh and Homan Avenue. Emmett always brings us news stories and gossip from the streets.

"Attorney General Palmer raided the labor unions to find the Bolsheviks."

"Armour & Company offered meat-packers raises and insurance for not joining unions."

"White strikers at The Union Stock Yard threw rocks at their own black strikers."

"A bomb destroyed Wentworth Apartments, killing a little black girl named Ernestine."

"A black man in Arkansas refused to get off the sidewalk and a mob lynched and shot him."

"A black pastor disappeared from Metcalfe, Mississippi, after Sunday services."

"Metcalfe?" Odell asks Emmett after he hears that news.

"That's over there by the Mississippi River. We been up that way," Emmett tells him. To Foster, he says, "You keep off the busy streets when you leave school. And go the long way to get here. We don't want no trouble."

Odell works with Emmett after school, emptying the wood garbage bins up and down the neighborhood, and he brings us treasures: A bicycle wheel with a bent rim. A crooked bowling pin. A chipped shaving mug.

He makes a great show of presenting these pearls to us, bowing and saying in his deep, soft voice, "May I present your majesties with a small token of my appreciation?" And we know Odell will tell us the story of the treasure once he gets ready.

One day we're just finishing catching some fish when

Odell and Emmett show up, Odell carrying a wrought-iron skillet with a crack smack down the middle of the handle. He plunks it down and then strips off his shirt to wash himself with river water. Getting rid of the rubbish-collecting stink. Right away we put some lard in the pan and start those fish a-frying. We throw in a couple stolen potatoes from Ma's larder and a swatch of bacon from one of Ma's meat packages from Mr. O'Doulle. I try to be generous when I can.

Then we ask Odell to tell the story of the frying pan

Odell turns the skillet over in his hands, tracing the crack with his finger.

"You got one to tell?" asks Foster, hope in his voice.

Emmett whispers, "Tell about Mama's bread."

Odell begins. "When you were nigh high to a grass-hopper, Mama plopped you up to the table while she was making dinner."

"Where were you and Emmett?" interrupts Foster.

"Shh. Let him tell it," says Emmett.

"And she gave you some raisins to keep you quiet."

"Sure wish we had some raisins every day," says Emmett.

"Shh," says Foster. "Let him tell it."

I can't help smiling. It's the same when Mary tells Anna a story. She always interrupts. 'Course she's only little, but still, I think, we all love the stories, don't we?

Odell leans close to the fire. His eyes tell the story just the same as his mouth. "So Mama, she whipped up the corn bread batter and poured it into the skillet. Then she set the skillet right there on the table while she heated up the stove. When she turned back for the skillet, there you were, covered in corn bread batter." Odell holds up his hands. "You dropped your raisins into the batter and then stuck your hands in, trying to fish them out again.

"At dinnertime, Mama says, 'Boys, we're having a new kind of bread tonight. Fosterbread.' We didn't understand until we took that first bite and found those raisins buried in each piece. And ever since then, us Williams's corn bread is called Fosterbread and it has raisins in it." Odell pokes Foster in his belly and we all laugh.

"My ma puts raisins in her scones sometimes," I say. My mouth waters thinking about chewy raisins in a scone slathered with butter.

"Do you call it Billyscone?" Odell pokes me too.

"Tell it again," says Foster, a wistful look in his eye and I know he's missing the meals his mama used to make when they all lived down South. I decide to give my ma an extra hug when I get home.

After the story, everything is quiet, except for the sounds in the woods. We hear a commotion above our heads and see the shapes of two squirrels balancing on a branch, busy chattering about something. A second later the sky starts falling, just like in the Chicken Little story. *Plop! Plop!* Little round balls fall off the tree, landing all around us and right in the fire.

Foster picks up one that lands close to his foot and holds it up for us to see: it's a hairy brown seed bigger than an acorn. "What is it?" he asks.

"Beechnut," says Emmett.

"Sort of a silly nut, if you ask me," says Odell, pointing at the nuts burning up in the fire.

Me and Foster split a gut laughing.

Just then a beechnut pops and jumps from the fire into the frying pan and Odell asks, "Now, what kind of nut goes and jumps from the fire into the frying pan?"

"A beechnut," we holler and bust up laughing again.

Odell points at us and raises his eyebrows. "Sounds like we got a couple of big beechnuts fell off the tree right here."

Every treasure Odell brings down to the creek has a story from down South, most often starring Foster, "nigh high to a grasshopper." But there're others about his family, too. I get to know Foster's sisters from the story of the chipped shaving mug, how they demanded their daddy lather their faces with shaving cream same as Foster, Odell, and Emmett. So he granted their wish, covering their whole face with shaving cream, only leaving their eyes. "I wasn't sure where your whiskers would start popping out," was their daddy's pretended excuse.

"Nettie and Iris sure are a couple of beechnuts," Foster says then, making us laugh even harder than the first time.

I also hear about their Uncle Jonas, who rode a bicycle for twenty miles to bring news that they had a new baby cousin, so excited he didn't even notice the bike had two flat tires by the time he jumped off and came running down the lane. Ever after they called him Uncle Flat.

"They shoulda called him Uncle Beechnut," says Foster. At school, when somebody does something ignorant, we whisper "Beechnut" to each other and smile. We're careful, though, not to be too chummy with each other at James Ward. I ain't no coward and I'm ready to prove it, but Foster tells me it ain't smart to be stupid.

"Billy, no sense making life hard for the both of us. It don't bother me none if we ignore each other at school. I don't put no never mind into what folks say anyway."

Ma thinks I'm hanging around with Timmy. And Timmy thinks I'm too busy to hang around 'cause I told him Miss Benson started giving lots of homework on account of summer break coming up in two months. I don't think he suspects anything. I'm playing both sides, hobnobbing with Timmy at church so he'll keep letting me work for his Da, and lazing around with Foster for no reason but that I enjoy being with him and his brothers, maybe more than ever I did with Timmy and my old chums.

But I do feel like a traitor. To Foster and to Timmy, even though he sure makes me mad sometimes. Holding on to the secret of my friendship with Foster so I don't make people mad, especially people like the Hamburgs. Like Mickey. If there's a way to be loyal to both, I can't figure it out.

Most days we walk by my house to drop off my glove and jacket before we head to the docks. The streets are usually empty so Foster don't got to worry, but he still acts a little skittish while he waits for me.

One Saturday I get an idea that we should have a secret hiding place where we can leave each other a message, like real spies do, and while Anna naps, I kneel down by the edge of the stairs. When I was little, I worked the stone loose and pretended there was an army graveyard behind it. I didn't know about war then. How 116,000 American soldiers would be killed in the Great War and lying in real graveyards. Now I'm glad to dig up that graveyard, scraping deeper into the mortar with my knife, until the hole gets as big as a half a loaf of bread.

The next Monday I show Foster. "Look here," I say. "You can put a message for me here. Or we can leave each other treasures."

"What treasure am I gonna have that you want?" Foster says in a doubtful voice.

"You might find something. Who knows? Promise you'll check every day, and I will too."

He nods, and we leave, take the long way to the docks and come up on the Twenty-Second Street Bridge. And just like that, we both feel the itching and know we got to climb it. At the top of the stairs we crawl out over the platform and swing our legs onto the roof. We can see for miles and miles, all the way to the downtown bridges and the lake, with the river below, just a hungry blue-gray snake waiting for us to fall in. The seagulls circle and dive like little white fighter planes.

"Did your daddy fly a plane in the war?" Foster asks.

"I don't know. I don't think so. Did yours?"

"Nah. Think it's scary?"

"Flying?"

"No, war."

"Yah. Yah, I do. But that don't matter. I'm going to be in the Field Artillery."

"Odell wants to join up, but he can't. Got his leg all mangled up picking cotton. And he's barely seventeen."

"Oh," I say. "What about Emmett?"

Foster laughs. "You know Emmett. He don't like trouble. Says he ain't interested in dying." He fishes in his pocket and pulls out a penny. Precious as it is, he throws it as far as he can.

"What'd you do that for?"

"Luck."

I fish in my pocket and fling my prized penny out even farther. "Whaddaya reckon would happen if somebody jumped off this bridge?"

"They'd be dead, probably. Wonder how deep it is," he says.

"If I knew it was deep enough, I'd dive right in," I brag.

I wait to hear Foster doubt me, to jeer like Timmy and say something like, "No you won't, you yellow chicken," but instead he just says, "Well, that'd be something. I'd climb up here just to watch. I bet you'd make a big splash and come up laughing."

We both laugh, and I'm glad we're friends.

Foster climbs down first and I follow. He swings down

to the little platform, but while I'm still on the bottom rung, I see a police car pull up.

"What you doing, boy?" A voice shouts from the open window. Then the door opens and a hand reaches out to grab Foster, who's just stepped to the curb.

Foster steps back out of reach and freezes. I scramble from behind the railing and jump off the platform, landing close to him.

"Hey." I say it loud and move just a little in front of Foster. Timmy and I climb this bridge all the time. Others, too, and nobody never bothered us about it.

I turn and whisper to Foster. "They don't recognize you. But they know me. It'll be okay, just watch."

The hand moves out of sight, back into the car, and the door shuts. The officer leans out the window and looks me right in the eye. "Does your ma know where you are? Or that you're out here with the likes of them?" His eyes look behind me, toward Foster, as he nods.

He pulls his head back inside. "You boys keep off that bridge, you hear? No trespassing. City property." Then the car speeds away.

Foster won't look at me and at first I puzzle to understand why. Is he mad we climbed the bridge? Mad I pushed in front of him? Mad 'cause they recognized me?

Then it comes to me. Because he's black the police started to make trouble. Because I'm white the trouble stopped. We are both who we are, me white, him black, and when we're together somebody is on the wrong side of the line.

Trespassing, the police said. It wasn't trespassing when the boys from Bridgeport climbed the bridge. It's getting clearer to me about that line. Some think people with black skin shouldn't be trespassing. Trespassing on the white ways, that's what the officer means.

If I was Foster I would be mad, too.

I feel embarrassed. Guilty. I wish we were all born one color. A dark color that don't sunburn. Being friends with Foster makes me sit up and take notice, like a dog that hears a noise. I'm ashamed I didn't notice before that. I'm ashamed it's come to this, when every day in school we stand up and pledge liberty and justice for all.

"It don't matter," I tell him. And I think about my da, standing up for that man at the parade. Am I crossing the line, like he said, or just showing off?

The day is slipping away, and work is waiting. We skedaddle off the bridge and to the docks, just stopping for Foster to buy a *Chicago Defender* newspaper for his daddy from a street vendor.

Mr. Weinstein leaves his *Chicago Tribune* on the table for me and Ma to read, but it ain't the same as *The Chicago Defender*. I catch a glimpse of the headline when Foster rolls it up:

TEXANS LYNCH PROMINENT BLACK DENTIST.

Chapter Five

EASTER COMES. WE GO TO church, dressed in our finest. We say a prayer for Ireland and the ones who lost their lives three Easters ago in the Easter Rising. Those poor souls who fought the British, wanting to be free. Ma reminds us again that Da's very own brother died in the Easter Rising. We say a prayer for his poor soul, too.

Timmy and his ma sit in the pew with us. Mrs. Beatty's Easter hat dips down low in the front, with a net over her eyes. I bet Ma wishes she had such a hat. Hers is plumb nothing compared to that big hat.

"What'd you do to your cheek?" I ask Timmy.

He puts his hand over the purple blush mark. "Nothing. I guess I fell."

"Bad luck," I say, but I know he didn't fall. Just like I know Mr. Beatty's been all night at the pub and that's why he ain't sitting in the pew next to his wife. It's been slow on the docks. People are riled up 'cause if there's no work, there's no money. No money, no food. But it seems there's always money for the poison.

"Me and Ma are going for the Easter give-outs at Hull House. Want to come?" Timmy hides his cheek when he turns to whisper to me.

"What give-outs?"

"Some Easter fixings. Da says it's charity and won't go, but Ma says it's just donations so there's no harm."

Ma gives me a poke to shut me up. I quick whisper back to Timmy, "I can't. We're going to see my da."

And anyway, the meat-packers where my da used to work sent over a nice ham for our Easter. Ma don't like charity either, but she sure wouldn't hit me if I wanted to go get some. I wish I could tell Foster and his brothers about the give-outs. Seems like the lot of them could use a good meal and give their auntie a break from cooking.

We eat our free ham for Easter dinner. Mr. Weinstein, our Russian spy, shares our meal, but he doesn't eat our ham and we don't eat the black bread he brings Ma for a gift. We each get two boiled eggs to put into dye and two chocolate eggs to put into our mouths. Mr. Weinstein holds his egg in his hand for a long time, staring at it with a sad expression, and Mary pokes me and raises her eyebrows. When Ma ain't watching, I stick one of each of the eggs in my pocket to put in the secret hiding spot for Foster. Just for a lark I checked behind the rock on Saturday morning and, don't you know, I found he left me a gray pebble with specks glittering inside it like stars.

On the way to visit Da, Ma gives me a brown package wrapped with twine, and sends me running over to Prairie Avenue while she and the girls loiter around the flowers in the park. It's a skirt she altered for Mrs. Helen Morris, the married daughter of Mr. Swift, who owns the biggest meat-packing company in The Union Stock Yards. Timmy says his da tried to get a job there too, but Mr. Swift started hiring black workers, paying 'em less money, and making 'em promise not to join the union. Sure doesn't seem fair to me. Not fair to nobody.

"Tell her I'm sorry for the inconvenience of a Sunday, but she needs it for Wednesday's White Sox game. Remember, Billy. 2036 Prairie. And wait for the money."

I light out down Michigan Avenue and then cut a few

blocks over to Prairie. And quick as a wink, I'm in a different world full of castle-looking houses and fancy cars. Boys in short pants and long socks ride shiny bicycles and girls with big bows play hopscotch in the middle of clean streets. The smell is fresh, no stink in it. Every house is bigger and more beautiful than the house before it. When I get to 2036 Prairie, I open the gate and walk to the white marble steps.

Then I stop. Do I go to the front door or around to the back? It don't seem like a good idea for the likes of me to be wandering around the property, but it don't seem like a good idea for me to waltz up to the front door and put my grimy hands on the brass door knocker. While I'm puzzling about it, the door opens.

"What you want?" A large black lady in a gray dress with a white apron looks down on me disapprovingly. *Must be their maid.* Gol dang but they're rich. Foster's auntie is a domestic in a big house like this.

"I'm making a delivery."

"On Easter Sunday?"

"Mrs. Morris told my ma she needs it for Wednesday." A girl Anna's size with black curls spilling about her shoulders holds onto the maid's dress. *Must be Mrs. Morris's daughter,* I think. Anna's hair is curly like that, but Ma keeps it short so the bugs can't live in it.

"Deliveries go to the back." The maid starts to shut the door but I hear another voice.

"What is it, Julia?" I see the door open again and a lady with a beehive basket hat on her head leans around the maid, pulling the little girl away. *Must be Mrs. Morris.* What Ma wouldn't give for that hat, silly as it is.

"Delivery, ma'am. I told him go 'round back." And the maid tries to shut the door.

"I'm fully capable of assessing the situation myself. Get on back to the kitchen." Mrs. Morris slaps the maid's hand off the door and pushes her back into the hall. Then she steps out. Her dress is layers of yellow fabric, with some rows of lacy flowers on the bottom and a shiny fat ribbon circling around her waist. Her dark hair peeks out from the hat, which I now notice has the same color yellow flowers on it.

"Domestic help is so difficult to manage," she says to me. "Can I help you?"

"Yes, ma'am," I say. "I'm delivering for my ma, Adelaide McDermott."

Mrs. Morris claps her hands together. "Oh, she finished. That's wonderful."

I dare to walk up the steps and hand her the package.

"And what's your name?" she says.

I can barely speak after I get a glimpse at the house through the cracked door. Even heaven don't look so grand, I'm sure. More furniture than a furniture store, and rugs covering the floors. "Billy," I start, then start again. "William Jarlath McDermott, ma'am."

"Well thank you, William." She turns, takes her daughter by the hand, and closes the door. I'm left standing on the steps, dumbfounded, for a minute. Then a thunderbolt knocks me upside the head. Gol dang it. Ma needs that money. Ain't it just like rich folks to stiff the poor? I rush to the door and bang on it.

The maid opens it a crack and don't look happy to see me.

"My ma told me to wait for the money," I say.

She don't answer me so I try again. "Tell Mrs. Morris my ma told me to wait for the money."

"Tell her yourself," the maid says to me in a scolding voice. She pushes the door all the way open and disappears.

I ain't rude as a general rule, but this has got my dander up. If I go off without the money, all my ma's hard work will be for nothing. And if I go hollering after this highfalutin lady, no telling what might happen. Just then the little girl sees me. "Go get your ma, will you?" I tell her. She doesn't move.

"Want to see something?" I tell her, the way I do with Anna.

She nods. I reach in my pocket and pull out the rock Foster left me in our secret place. She smiles. "Go get your ma and you can have it," I tell her, and she runs down the hall. A few minutes later, Mrs. Morris returns, following her little girl.

"I'm sorry, ma'am. My ma told me to wait for the money." I look at my toes when I say this, afraid she might slap me or push me like she did the maid.

"Oh, how silly of me. I was going to drop it by the post office, but this is easier," she says. She reaches into a wooden box on the table by the door and pulls out two bills. I quick stuff them in my pocket and put the rock on the doorstep.

And then I fly out of there. If only we could have one of them rugs, we could sell it and eat for a month. And on account of these people, the blacks can't join the unions and make equal wages with the whites. Don't that beat all?

After, when we visit Da, I want to ask him about rich and poor. How did it get to be so unequal? I want to ask him about Joe Jackson. Is he mad at Joe for dodging the draft? I want to ask him about Mr. Weinstein. What should I do if he's a Russian spy? I want to ask him about lynching. Why do people hate so much they kill? And mostly I want to ask him about being friends with Foster. Is it something to be proud of, like I sometimes think? Or am I taking a risk for no reason?

But he just nods and smiles and pats Anna on the head. His chocolate egg lies in his lap, uneaten. He never says a word and I don't either. Like Odell says, it ain't worth wasting the bait if there ain't fish in the water. So I just look him straight in the eye and think what I would say if he could hear me.

We bundle up and wave goodbye, my unasked questions settling back into the hole in my heart. I take one more look at Da and a fist of fear starts to strangle all my good feelings.

We walk to the trolley stop on State Street. The lake is behind us, the wind pushing us to hurry. Anna skips. Mary holds her head up, flouncing her hair. She didn't even try to talk to Da. Just folded her arms over her chest and stared out the window until the visit was over. I know she and Da didn't get on so good, but seeing how he suffers, would it hurt Mary to give him a smile?

We get off at Twenty-Second Street 'cause Ma needs a quart of milk, and she sends me running over to Anderson's on the corner. I like Anderson's, owned by a black man named Charles B. Anderson. They treat me nice, like I'm an important customer. Da used to buy the oysters for the parish fair at Anderson's, on account of the ladies won't make the oyster stew with anybody else's oysters.

When Da used to take us to the beach, we always stopped by Anderson's for bottles of Coca-Cola.

Today, the men out front nod at me. The man behind the counter says, "Where y'all been? Where's Red?" That's what he calls my da. He remembers me, and I ain't been here in two years.

"At St. Luke's Hospital. Back from the war."

"Well, you tell him to get better and get on back here."

He rings up the milk and points to the stick candy. "Pick one out for you and little blue eyes. And you better get one for your high-and-mighty sister, too." He means Big Bossy, of course. She always waits at the door of Anderson's on account of the bait they sell stinks. She says it's disgusting. Da used to tell her she better get used to it 'cause he planned to marry her off to a fisherman who lived above a bait shop. I laughed my head off, but Mary didn't. I might just leave her candy for Foster in our secret hiding spot. He don't act all high and mighty.

One time I asked my da why the kids stare at us so hard when we go into Anderson's.

"Cause we're different from them. Blue eyes and freckles."

"But I don't stare and they're different from me."

"If you ain't staring, then how you know they're staring at you?" My da laughed at me. Then he said, "Different is good, Billy. Smart people, they learn to love different."

"How do you get smart, Da?"

"My da, the one whose name you got, told me of a great black man, Frederick Douglass, who visited my Grandda O'Connell on my mother's side in Dublin. He and this Mr. Douglass talked about freedom together. They both believed all of us, rich and poor, on both sides of the ocean, all of us should be free. Listening to smart people makes us smart, Billy. Believing we can stand up for what we believe, too."

We wait for the next trolley. It's April but our hands feel mighty cold holding the candy up to our mouths, and we hop on right quick when it stops for us. The trolley turns on Halsted and stops in front of Schaller's Pump. We get out. A couple of blokes whistle at Mary. Ma yells at them to mind their manners. Some important-looking men in suits climb out of a black car and some of the Hamburgs rush to open the pub door for them. As we go round the corner I see Timmy with Mickey and his Hamburg boys, and I pull my cap down low, remembering the mean word on my essay, and how Ma don't want me hobnobbing with the likes of Mickey.

"Where ya going, Billy?" says Timmy and he comes running over.

"I got work to do."

"We got some work for you here. It's okay with you isn't it, Mrs. McDermott?"

I can see Ma turning it over in her head. She don't like Mickey, but she's friends with Timmy's ma and she don't want Timmy spreading it around that my ma is too proud to let me do a little work for the Hamburgs. Besides, she's thinking that doing a favor for the Hamburgs is a bird in the hand while Da's holed up in the hospital.

"Get home before dark," she says and hustles Mary and Anna along.

And Ma doesn't know it, but she just volunteered me to run liquor for the next two hours to secure votes for Judge Landis and Mayor Thompson.

"You gotta give the money to Mickey or Dynamite Joey. You know Joey—his da sponsors the Hamburgs. Then they'll split with us." Timmy talks tough, a cigarette hanging from his teeth. I think he looks ridiculous.

The labor bosses are inside with the mayor, he explains.

White folks are mad at Thompson because he promised to help black folks if they vote for him. "He's trying to make his peace with us white folks," Timmy says. "The dockers and the meat-packers say they won't vote for Thompson because he's siding with the blacks. He can't win if he don't get the meat-packers and the dockers. That's why we're giving them these bags. If he don't get their votes, then he may as well pack his sorry you-know-what down south." It's Timmy talking, but it's his da's words that tumble out.

Mickey gives me a wink and a nod when he hands me and Timmy four bags with a bottle in each. We carry them to bungalows between Bubbly Creek and Nativity of Our Lord. Always the same message: "Compliments of the mayor, reminding you to vote next Tuesday."

Our last delivery takes us to Wentworth, close to the Black Belt. Close to where I think Foster and his family might live. The whole crowd of us stays together on this run, and I notice the Hamburg boys seem pretty corked up. I ain't never had a drop of drink, and I know Timmy stays clear on account of his da's problem. But Mickey and Joey keep nipping from a bottle, shouting out swears, and yelling at everybody.

Mothers and fathers pull their little ones out of our way. Young ladies hurry past, embarrassed by the wolf whistles.

We make the delivery, but Mickey still carries one last bag, which he sips from every so often.

Mickey stops and I turn to follow his eyes. On the other side of Wentworth, two black boys are playing with a puppy.

Mickey whistles and the puppy trots out to the middle of the street. "Hey boy, ain't that your dog?" he yells to one of the boys.

Eyes wide, the boys stare at us.

"I said, ain't that your dog? You better get that mutt out of my street." He pulls the bottle from the bag and the sinking sun flashes off the gold liquor.

Joey says, "Rip his bleedin' head off."

Timmy whoops. The others laugh. Mickey glances at his audience. The fists of fear twist my heart and I want to turn away, but I can't. I want to say, "Stop," but I can't. What if something bad happens? What if Foster's taking a walk after Sunday dinner and he sees me here?

One of the boys, the littler one, makes a sound at the puppy with his lips and takes a few steps into the street. The puppy turns and wags its tail. Mickey whistles again and pulls part of a sandwich from his pocket. He throws it into the street.

The puppy turns back and takes steps toward the

sandwich, the little boy following, begging it to come back. Just when the boy reaches the puppy, Mickey whips the bottle.

I turn and run fast toward home. The sounds come after me. The crash of the bottle. The squeal of the puppy. The scream of the boy.

Mickey's stabbing words chase after me as I run. "Where you goin', N—— lover?"

And with each footstep, my own voice whispers, "Coward. Coward. Coward."

Chapter Six

I'M PRETTY SURE SISTER SALMONETTI never heard of Tom Sawyer, his morals being fairly corrupt and all, so reading the book at James Ward is new to me, and it sure is grand. I mull over his adventures every day while I heft boxes and barrels onto the waiting wagons. Miss Benson told us that in Mark Twain's next book, Tom and Huck are friends with Jim, a black man. No one gets mad at them. No one calls them names.

I remember one time, when me and my da was walking in Grant Park, I sat down on a bench to tie my shoe. On one end of the bench sat a black man. A man with a dog walked by and yelled at my da, "Hey, Red, don't your boy know any better?"

But I didn't know better and my da explained to me, "That man don't like you sitting on the bench with a black man."

"Why? What's wrong with him?" I asked.

"Billy," my da said, "some people just don't have any sense. They judge by the cover. They think it's the outside that tells about the inside, but it ain't so. You know, Billy, there's a saying in Ireland: 'Under the shelter of each other, we survive.' We depend on each other, Billy. Promise me you'll not judge a book by its cover."

I didn't half understand, but I nodded.

Then he winked at me. "Walk straight, my son, as the old crab said to the young crab." And he laughed. Oh, but I loved his laugh.

It still puzzles me, how people sit in church and say the Our Father but throw bottles at boys and puppies. How we're proud of the Civil War but lynch the very people that was rescued from slavery. I wish again for my da to be home to explain it.

One day at the end of April a crate tips off the wagon when a horse rears up, right open. It breaks open, spilling everything into the gutter. Later, after I sneak to Foster's fort, I present the treasure I pulled from the street: a smoked ham shank covered in sawdust and mud. Odell washes it in the creek and Emmett fixes it onto a roasting spit over the fire. We're drooling from the smell, and chase off two dogs that wander down the path, led by their noses.

Finally we eat ham, glorious ham, until we can't stand the sight of it. Odell asks if I have a story to tell in honor of the ham.

"No, you go."

Odell puts his chin in his hand and thinks for a spell. I love to see his eyes twinkle when he's thinking up a story.

"Well, this is the story of the ham," he says. "Down South, Easter Day always brings the relatives together. Mama gets on her high horse, making everybody shine their shoes, and lay out their Sunday best."

"Don't forget to put me in the story," Foster interrupts, as usual.

Odell winks. "Let's see. Are you in this story?" He closes his eyes again.

"Oh-day-all!" Foster pulls Odell's name out and up in the middle.

Odell says, "Oh, yes. You are in the story. I forgot. And guess what? You were—" He stops and waits.

"Nigh high to a grasshopper," we both shout, me knowing the line from hearing so many of the stories. Someday, maybe I'll tell stories to Anna. Stories about the funny things she did, and the way Da used to be.

Odell goes on, "So this Easter, we teach Fozzy to say Happy Easter. But he just can't get it quite right. 'Hay Ear.' That's what it sounded like. So when we get to church, Foster, in his short pants and bow tie, parades straight into church, saying, 'Hay Ear' to everybody, grinning from ear to ear himself, pleased as punch when all our aunties make a fuss over him:

"'Isn't he cute?'

"'Such a little man.'

"'If he isn't a little ham?'

"'That's right, he's a little ham.'"

"I did not wear short pants," Foster says with an indignant tone.

"Shh. Yes you did," says Emmett.

"The preacher finally finishes, and we go home. Mama and the womenfolk get busy in the kitchen cooking up a storm for Easter dinner and Foster keeps close by, hoping for some nibbles. Grandmama wasn't feeling too good, her health just starting to go downhill. So Mama says, 'Mama, what do you feel like? You want me to make you something? Scrambled eggs?'"

"'No, honey, no. I'll just eat a little ham,' she says.

"And there was Foster, standing in the door, his ears sharp as a fox. All of a sudden, he bolts out the door and runs off across the yard. And all the folk in the kitchen come out to see that little ham running to beat the band, heading to hide in the bushes."

Odell grabs hold of Foster's knee. "It took Daddy and Emmett to fetch you and drag you back to the house, all the time you crying, 'I'm not a little ham. Don't let nobody eat me.'"

Oh golly. I can't help hooting. And I laugh even harder at Foster's face. I can tell he's never heard this story before. He's trying so hard not to laugh he keeps sputtering.

"Want a little ham, Fozzy?" asks Odell, pointing to the leftovers.

Finally Foster's eyebrows lift up and he lets the smile back on his face. "Is that a true story?" he asks.

"True as the gospel," says Emmett.

"True as steel," says Odell.

"True as buying a pig in a bag. That's what the Irish say," I add.

Everybody laughs.

"That's a good one, Billy. A pig in a poke and the ham in the little ham," says Emmett.

"Better than being a beechnut!" says Foster, folding his arms across his chest.

"Gol dang," I say appreciatively. It's the best story yet, and we beg to hear it again.

Odell obliges us and we drink in his deep, low, voice, watching his eyes shine in the firelight as the sun goes away from the sky.

Odell is really something. He's never said a word to me that ain't kind, but whenever Emmett brings news about lynchings his face shows he's burning inside. When Foster and me do our homework in the lean-to, he explains it best he can, but not in a know-it-all way. And even though he works with Emmett after school, he always beats Emmett to the lean-to so he can hang around with us. Foster tells me all the girls in Jackson, Mississippi, are sweet on Odell.

"Like bees to the honey pot," Foster said. "But he don't pay them no never mind. And that makes 'em swarm even worse."

Emmett can get a little bossy, reminding me of someone else I know. He wants to sound all important, bringing us the gossip and stories, but he don't want to join up for the NAACP meetings—maybe 'cause he's such a light color, figuring he can get by if he don't ruffle feathers in Chicago.

"Turtles don't get their heads chopped off unless they stick out their necks," he tells Foster and Odell when they argue about things still being unfair for black people.

Then he tells us all about the thirty-six bombs mailed from New York to important government people. He knows more details than were in the *Tribune*. The first man to receive a bomb unwrapped the brown paper to find a box wrapped in bright green paper and marked GIMBELS SAMPLES.

I bet he was mighty glad he didn't read that day, because he didn't see the words OPEN HERE and he opened the wrong end, so the bottle of acid dropped out onto the table instead of onto the blasting caps that trigger the dynamite. He brought the box to the police and they went to the post office to warn them. Thank goodness, sixteen of the thirty-six boxes hadn't had enough postage, so the postmaster hadn't mailed them. And they recovered the others before they did any damage.

My mind starts racing back to Mr. Weinstein and the powder, the wires, and the box he took out of the car. I'm pretty sure what I saw was the makings of a bomb. I promise myself that, come heck or high water, I will find a way to investigate.

It's Foster who first has the idea of the raft, the ham reminding him of Tom and Huck and Joe—how they steal a raft, eat ham, and run away to a pirate island. We mull it over, the ham making our stomachs fat and full.

By the time the factory whistle blows at six o'clock, it's settled. I will bring an ax. Emmett will be on the lookout for baling twine on his garbage runs. He says he's seen some railroad ties behind the Albert Pick & Company warehouse we might drag down. Only Odell is quiet on the subject.

"You can bring a tarp," I tell him. "Tom had a tarp."

"We ain't gonna put this thing in the water," he replies.

"Course we're gonna put it in the water. How will we know if it floats?" I tell him.

"We can't. Ain't none of us learned to swim."

I gape, big as life. What knucklehead ain't learned to swim? Heckfire. We're boxed in by water. Lake Michigan to the east and the Chicago River to the north. Not to mention this here Bubbly Creek tickling our toes. And didn't Foster's family grow up fishing in Jackson, Mississippi?

I been swimming like a tadpole since my da threw me in the lake when I was three. Gol dang and saints preserve us. But Odell isn't joking. His eyes have the same look as when I told him about the boy and the puppy a few weeks ago. Anxious. Worried. I get a feeling that the raft isn't a good idea after all, leastways not until I teach them all to swim, and I'm about to say so.

But before I can, Foster slaps Odell's knee. "Well, Beechnut, you best not fall off the raft."

We laugh and Odell grabs Foster, rubbing his knuckles across his scalp.

"You better say 'Uncle,'" I say.

"Why?" Foster squirms and Odell rubs harder.

"'Cause then he'll stop. Ain't you never heard of that?"

"Not in Mississippi. Okay, okay. Uncle, uncle."

"Odell, you gotta let up," I say. "He said 'Uncle.'"

Foster twists away, and Odell grabs me and starts rubbing my head. "We do things different in the South, Billy Boy."

Foster swoops in and tickles Odell until he shouts, "Uncle. Uncle."

When I walk home that day I think about wee little Baby Brian, my brother who never even made it home from the hospital, and I wish I could be a big brother to him, like Odell is to Foster.

As I cross over the bridge at Halsted, I hear a splash in the river, and my heart jumps. It worries me, making me think of Mickey and the puppy, the breaking glass, and the yell of the boy. Odell's face when he told me he couldn't swim, haunted-looking, flashes in my memory. They gotta learn to swim, all right, but maybe there's worse fears than

95

drowning. Maybe the raft might come in handy someday if Mickey and his friends come sniffing around, throwing bottles at more innocent people.

Chapter Seven

WE WORK ON THE RAFT all through May. We got a good start, but it still don't look like much. Emmett brought home part of a steel cable, and we looped it in half and attached it to a rope, then knotted the rope around a little tree up in the woods, near the path. That way, we figure, even if a storm washes away the trees on the creek bank, the raft on its leash might not float away.

I don't go to Bubbly Creek every day. In fact, I try to be sneaky about it, only going every couple of days, in case Timmy gets suspicious. Some days I walk home with him and his da, unless they're heading to the club.

Timmy's always talking about Mickey and the Hamburgs, and I wonder if he's really as much a regular as he makes it sound.

"Remember when we toted that liquor all around to remind folks to vote for the mayor? Remember how folks were so mad cause he was making promises to the blacks, telling them he's their brother?" Timmy dances around me punching the air, like a boxer. "Well, Big Bill lied about those promises to blacks. Now we know now he just made promises so they'd vote for him like they did last time. Mickey says he even refused to meet with a real important black lady, somebody named Ida Wells, and her committee to talk about the bombings in the black neighborhoods."

I read the papers every day. I know what they say about Big Bill Thompson. "Sure. He went around promising *everybody* everything."

"Yah, well, you see any blacks living in better houses, going to better hospitals, or getting better jobs?" says Timmy.

I'm careful what I say to Timmy. It's clear Mickey and his boys keep a watchful eye for what goes on in the neighborhood and that keeps us safe, but sometimes Timmy and his Hamburgs make me so mad. Always picking on black folks. He don't like Jews, Italians, Poles, or Mexicans either. He even called Ma a commie traitor once because Mr. Weinstein is our boarder.

"I don't see anybody with better anything," I say. "Your da is still looking for a job and my da is still in the hospital. It's bad times for all folks."

"That's because the blacks are taking over the bleedin' city. Mickey says we need to teach them a lesson. They all need to move back down south where they belong. He says we aim to show them how bad it's going to be. That spy living in your house better watch out, too. You'll all go to jail if he's caught, you know." Timmy's voice is pitchy from getting all worked up. He's got a crop of pimples on his chin and the littlest bit of hair above his lip.

It scares me, the way his face changes when he talks like that.

"Aw, come on, Timmy," I say. "Let's worry about the White Sox. Think they'll make it to the Series? They got a good start."

He calms down. Every time we walk home from the docks together I been turning the talk to my White Sox, who by the end of May have twenty-four wins and seven losses. Twenty-four wins! Oh my Sally! Gol dang.

Some days I light out early from work and stop by the Woolworth Five and Dime to spend the jingle in my pocket: a candy for Anna, a pencil for Mary, hand cream for Ma, and of course baseball cards for me.

Some days I pop in to see Mr. O'Doulle and he sends me off to deliver brown paper packages to Herman's Diner or Lee's Place.

On one of those days he comes from behind the counter, wiping his hands on his apron. "How's your ma, Billy?"

"Working something fierce," I say.

"Have you given any thought to what you'll do once school's out? I could sure use quick feet and honest hands to make deliveries this summer."

I don't know what to say. When school's out? I ain't thought about summer coming.

"If you were a regular delivery boy, I could pay you a bit, and send some of the meat ends home for your ma." He takes a package the size of my baseball glove from the top of the case and puts it in my arms. "Cut these too thin for my last customer. See if your ma can make use of them."

"Thanks, Mr. O'Doulle. I will."

"Will you let me know about delivering?" he says as he walks behind the counter.

"Sure, sure I will," I say. I can almost hear the coins dropping into my Wise Pig bank. When I walk out into the sunshine, I remember what summer used to be like, going to the beach and the ball games with my da. But now? I need to keep helping my family out. Will Timmy and his da still go to work on the docks in the summer? Even these days, sometimes we try to work but just stand around with nothing to do. And it won't be easy to sneak off to Bubbly Creek to finish the raft during the summer, with the Hamburgs keeping an eye on the neighborhood. I guess making deliveries might be the only way to bring in some earnings. I have to give it some thought, or I might go crazy stuck with Big Bossy and Crybaby all day.

All through the last week of school, it rains and rains. The river rises until it's just below the dock and floods its banks. Bubbly Creek overflows and washes away our fire pit and some materials we'd been saving for the raft. There's no trace of the rocks we usually stand on for fishing.

It rains the day before our last day of school and me and Foster head straight to the creek, knowing there ain't no work at the docks. We ain't played baseball in ages with all this rain, and now with summer coming I don't know how we'll all get together.

"It's looking good for our White Sox," I tell him as we half run, half walk along.

"Good. What's their record?" he asks.

"Twenty-four to seven. First place," I say.

"Yah? Keen. The Chicago Giants are in second."

"The Giants? Who's that?"

"You know, the black players' leagues," Foster says. "They're good."

I don't want to argue with him, but I doubt some unknown league could be as good as the White Sox, so I change the subject. "Emmett say anything more about the bombs? Did they catch the communists?"

"Nope, but he said they're suspecting just about everybody."

"Want to know something?" I whisper. "But you can't tell."

"What?" Foster whispers back and stops walking.

I glance around, then lean close to him. "We got a spy, right in our house, in my old bedroom!"

"Your very own communist? Living right under everybody's noses? That's keen. Keen as mustard."

"I'm getting ready to raid his room as soon as school's out. If I find anything I'll put it in our secret hiding spot," I tell him.

When we get to the lean-to we squeeze into the back, way out of the rain, which is slowing to a drizzle, and sit hunched over our homework, me doing sums and Foster writing something in a notebook.

"What're you working on? We didn't get a writing assignment, did we?" I ask.

"Nah, it's a letter."

"Who's it to?"

"My mama."

"Why? Can't you just go see her?"

"My mama's still down South with my sisters, Nettie and Iris."

"Down South? All this time I thought they was at your auntie's," I say, not pleased he let me believe that.

"No, I never said they were there. I just never said they weren't there," Foster says. "We came along first, to get things settled, after Daddy got in trouble for wearing his army uniform on the street. My daddy sends them money."

"Don't they want to come now? You've been gone a long time." It's mean to say, but sometimes I wish my sisters, Big Bossy and Crybaby, lived down South.

Odell slides into the lean-to, beads of water in his hair, and says hello, then relaxes just under the edge of the lean-to with his legs folded up, reading a book.

Foster carefully rips the letter out of his notebook and folds it perfectly. "Well, my daddy ain't sure it's safe yet and besides, my auntie says there ain't no work for women."

"'Course it's safe. Ain't nothing much happening in

Chicago." But I know that's not true. Things are happening. More every day. I think about the boy and the puppy, Foster and the bridge, and little Ernestine killed by a bomb. But at least there ain't no lynchings in Chicago. So that's a little safer, ain't it?

"What're you gonna do when school's out?" I ask Foster.

"We goin' down South."

Odell stops reading and turns to talk to us. "I don't think we're going, Foster."

"What about Mama? Nettie and Iris? And Grandmama and Paw-Paw? Daddy told me I'd see them in the summer." Foster scooches closer to Odell and I follow.

Odell is quiet after Foster's question. He picks up a stick lying close to the lean-to and pokes it in the soft mud, making patterns of circles with the holes. All we hear's the sound of the rain and the creek water rushing. Emmett isn't back from work and it's just the three of us, squished into the shelter.

"Billy," Odell says to get my attention.

"What?"

"Now you listen to me. I don't hate white people. I want you to know that before I tell Foster why we ain't goin' down South."

I stop fiddling with my shoelace. Odell's voice is full of muscle, and a little anger.

"Do you know what Jim Crow is, Billy? It's why we left Jackson. It's laws that white folks make for black folks. The color line. Like separate places to sit. Not being allowed some places where whites go."

"Why don't they stop Jim Crow making those laws?"

Odell lets out a short laugh, but he's not smiling. "Jim Crow's not a him. It's just the name they give the laws. From a song a long time ago, 'Jump Jim Crow,' where a white man makes fun of slaves. Down South, things are segregated—separate, you know? And if something goes wrong, black folks get punished."

"Everybody gets punished if they break the law."

"No, Billy. Not like that. Let's say I'm picking cotton and instead of paying me thirty cents a pound, they only give me half of what they owe me. What should I do?"

"Tell them to pay you what they owe you."

"I did." Odell pulls up the leg of his pants. Above his knee I see two raised scars the size of half dollars.

"Just for telling them to pay you?"

Odell leans toward me with an evil look in his eye. His voice gets even deeper. "'Oh, no, boy. You ain't been pickin' full baskets. You done slacked off. Eyes all around for the pretty ladies. You keep your black eyes on those cotton balls and off them white lilies.'" Odell spits the words out.

"I picked more cotton than anyone. And it was the owner's daughter waved at me, not the other way round."

"Didn't you tell them?" My voice comes out like a blue jay's cry, too loud and squawky. Odell's words and face scare me. There must be another reason for such rotten luck.

"Sure. I tried. Mr. Osborne jabbed me with a pitchfork and twisted my leg. But I was lucky. A farm worker in Waco, Texas, got burned and hanged this week. And they dragged a man out of a revival meeting in Georgia and lynched him."

"But that's in the South, ain't it? It's okay here in Chicago," I say. "I'm glad you ain't down there."

I get a prickle down my neck and the back of my mind nags at me: *But what about that time on the bridge when the policeman grabbed Foster? And what about that little girl who got bombed right out of her bed? Who will protect all the black people, if Mayor Thompson was lying?*

I feel surer than ever that I should be careful, pay attention, warn my friends. Like my da says. Look out for them and not be a coward. But how? Maybe read more in the paper. Maybe get me a subscription to *The Chicago Defender* and figure out the truth.

Foster puts a hand on Odell's arm, and there's a whine in his voice as he says, "But Odell, we ain't goin' back to work in Jackson, just visit. And Billy's right. It's not like down South here. Me and Billy go to school together, and most people don't pay us no mind."

Should I remind him about the ugly writing on my essay, and the police on the bridge? Tell him what Timmy and his da say? Or about Mickey's warning? But I'm scared saying it out loud might be unlucky. Me and Foster, we're the same. Is it wrong for us to want the world to be the way we want it to be?

"Really? Most people don't pay you no never mind?" Odell's voice comes out like coffee without sugar, accusing. "What about all the black people living over on Fifty-Fourth Place? One of them gangs, Ragen's Colts, 'didn't pay them no never mind,' sure. They shot out their streetlights, and busted up all their windows and doors. And guess when the police come to help out? After the damage was all done and the gang's gone away. We came to Chicago for opportunity, not to be scared all the time that something will break loose. It don't matter if white people associate with us. That ain't the point. The point is to be treated equal," says Odell. He pulls his long legs up and wraps his arms around them, leaning his chin on his knees.

"What about the boll weevil? That's why Daddy said he wanted to leave," Foster whines again.

Odell shushes him. "Yes, Fozzy, the boll weevil was eatin' the cotton. True. But the boll weevil wasn't attacking the people. Daddy calls it dis-en-fran-chise-ment." He draws out the word. "Losing land we bought and paid for. Sharecropping. The Klan stealing around, butchering blacks." Soft-spoken Odell spits these words out, a wrinkle between his eyebrows, his lips curled up in a sneer. The words must taste bitter to him, like the cod-liver oil Ma gives me in winter.

"In the South, Billy, the hate is floatin' on top of the water." Odell holds his hands out to me, dangling them in the air. "But in Chicago, the hate is like them rocks in the river. When there's plenty of water, you can't see 'em." And with a jerk, Odell's hands squeeze into tight fists. He pushes them under my nose, staring at me, until I look away.

He turns to Foster. "It's low water now, Fozzy. Pa says it's a bad time. Bad to be traveling. Bad to be throwing good money after bad."

"But Daddy promised me. He'll change his mind. You'll see."

"Maybe, Fozzy. Maybe."

The rain stops. Only the drips from the leaves patter on the top of the lean-to.

Foster and I crawl out of the shelter and stand up on the edge of the creek bank, surveying the damage from the flooding. Bubbly Creek ate up our little beach, overflowing its bank, but even as we watch, the water goes down and we can see more of the gravelly sand. Branches of nearby trees bow into the water, and the river swirls around them, stealing their leaves.

Our raft ain't where we left it. Now it bobs ten feet out into the creek, still leashed to the little tree by its cable.

"Looks like she made it," Foster says.

"Yah. But that side came apart. We should fix it before the railroad tie comes loose."

Odell helps us pull the raft out of the water and stand it on its side to drip dry. We set to work piling up the stuff we need.

That's when Emmett shows up, soaking wet from collecting rubbish in the rain. "Hey y'all. Look." He sets a wooden crate down. It's a good and solid crate, the kind they use to ship fruit.

So far we've nailed together three partly rotten railroad ties we got up by the dock, and five sawed-off telephone poles that we rolled down the slope from the Albert Pick & Company warehouse.

It's hard to explain how the raft looks. The railroad ties

are all pointed one way with the poles in between them. They're not all even, and it's not level on the ground, but in the water it's fine.

On the top we used some twine to tie some skinnier trees and branches across everything, and we nailed down some flat boards we can sit on. Foster always has big ideas, like adding seats, or boxes to keep stuff in, or a tent like Tom Sawyer slept in.

But pounding nails and cutting cables takes longer than we imagine, so Foster's big ideas have to wait. Each time we think a new piece is about to fit, it's too skinny or too wide or it juts up, making the raft uneven. Or worse, somebody drops a nail and we spend fifteen minutes hunting for it.

Now that the top is a bit dry, we tip the raft flat again and maneuver it into the water. Emmett hands us the crate. He ceremoniously turns it around to show us the label, and we gasp.

It's brand-new–looking, dark-blue–bordered, and the picture shows golden yellow pears with fancy writing scrolled over the top. PRIDE OF THE RIVER. SACRAMENTO RIVER BARTLETTS. Next to the pears is a big riverboat, float-ing down a wide river in the sunset, with mountains in the background. In the corner, in red writing, it says, GROWN AND PACKED BY C.W. LOCKE & SON, LOCKE, CALIFORNIA.

We're in awe. It's perfect. Foster runs his hand over the label and lets out a big breath. "Keen!" he says.

Emmett grins. "Pride of the River," he says.

Foster fingers the name on the crate. "Locke & Son, Locke, California," he says. "It must be something to have a town named after you."

"Well, Foster John Williams. Just might be a town with your name someday." Odell splays his hands across the sky. "F. J. Williams, Williams, Illinois."

"The J is for my daddy's name, John," Foster tells me. "What's your middle name, Billy?"

I make a face. "Jarlath. After my grandda in Ireland."

Foster laughs. "Jeepers. Good thing William is your first name."

"Well, W. J. McDermott. You might have a town, too," says Odell.

"Best friends should share a town, don't you think?" says Foster. "How 'bout McWilliams? Or Willdermott?"

"Yah. Wouldn't that be something?"

We're best friends, all right, I think. But in my heart I know we're best friends in a private, sneaky kind of way. Like part of our friendship spends time in a secret hiding spot. If I was to walk on over to Foster's part of town, he'd likely pay me no never mind, just the same as I'd ignore him if he came to Mass at Nativity of Our Lord. We have an understanding that way, I think. Not wanting to stir up any hornet's nests. And there's plenty of hornet's nests out there. What if Mary told her shadow boy, Joey, and he told Mickey? What if Timmy told his da? It ain't that I'm stuck up, I'm just looking out for my family and my job. I got a lot to lose if those hornets start stinging.

And Foster? He needs to be careful out on his own. But what does he got to lose with me being his friend? He's even a little safer, maybe. That boy who used to make him pay a sandwich to cross the street don't bother him no more, now that I'm walking with him. Course, we separate a block before we come up on the docks, because, like I said, Timmy's da's got a mighty sharp stinger.

I remember how, one day in school, me and Foster worked on a project and before we turned it in, the teacher asked us to write our initials at the bottom. I wrote B and Foster wrote F.

Smarty-pants Helen peeked over our shoulders and pointed. "That could stand for Best Friends." But nobody was listening. Nobody usually listens to Helen.

Foster says it's fate for us to be friends, since we both have William in our names and our initials stand for Best Friends. And we agreed to be blood brothers, without the blood. I wish it could be the way Timmy and me used to be, but it's hard to be best friends and blood brothers when he can't come in my house, and I ain't never been invited to his.

Some days I wish that raft could carry us away, just like Huck Finn and Tom Sawyer. Away from Chicago, before those hate rocks start showing up everywhere, coming up to the surface like a rotten egg, ready to bust.

Mickey says they're going to teach them blacks a lesson. Odell says change is coming—change that will be bad. Emmett says it'll all blow over if we don't poke our heads up. Maybe they're all wrong. Maybe things will change for the better. Maybe it just takes time.

And right now our time is ticking away and we've got loads to do. Rebuild the fire pit. Collect more branches. And put our Pride of the River crate on the raft.

Odell sets it down on the raft. "Here, on the front?" he asks.

"That's the back," Foster says.

Emmett says, "The front will be whichever way the water wants it to be, so just put it anywhere."

"What's your middle name, Odell?" I ask.

"William. Odell William Williams."

I bust out laughing. "What? Well, that's plumb confusing."

"Nah. Easy to remember if you're not stupid, William Jarlath McDermott." He bonks me on the head. "Same as my dad's middle name. John William Williams."

"Well," I say, punching him back, "I suppose you could take your wife's name when you get married. That way you could have three different names." I run to the other side of the raft.

"You little cotton picker." Odell lights out after me, and I splash into the water, daring him to follow, but he just laughs and kicks water up, daring me to come close.

Just then Foster cries out, "Would you look at that?"

I turn around and wade back toward the shore. In the middle of the creek, no more than ten feet from the raft, bobs a dead cow, bloated up like a balloon. Twigs and leaves swirl and jostle behind it, caught in the river traffic jam.

"Don't let it hit the raft," I yell.

"Is it dead?" Foster asks.

"Tarnation, it stinks." Odell grabs one of the poles just in case.

Emmett says, "Everybody, get out of the water."

We stand frozen, quietly disgusted, watching as the carcass drifts to a stop just beyond the raft. Stuck in the shallows, swollen and awful.

Foster's eyes are big. "That bird's getting a ride," he whispers, pointing.

"No. It's a crow. It's eating it." Emmett grabs a rock and aims for the crow, and the spell is broken.

"Ew," we all shout, and we grab rocks and sticks.

We're making a ton of noise. Yelling and pointing. Splashing. Throwing rocks and sticks at the monster.

But in that moment I feel something odd. Something wrong. I look around. See a flash of blue up near the path. A black cap. A face. Someone watches. Sees us. Sees me. I'm sure of it. I look closer. I blink and he's gone.

But I keep my mouth shut. Not wanting to worry everybody. Not wanting our fun to be over.

And, when I turn back, the cow sweeps past, finally caught in the current, with more debris from the flood.

Chapter Eight

WHAT A LETDOWN. JUNE'S HERE. School's out. And the first thing Ma says is, "Billy, Mary has a summer job so you'll be watching Anna for me." I can't help but blame my da. I shouldn't, I know, but if he would just buck up and get back to work all our lives would go back to normal. I guess I'll have to tell Mr. O'Doulle I ain't going to be able to be his errand boy.

Three days go by and every day I sit for Anna. I practice shooting marbles. I read the parts of *Tom Sawyer* that I skipped the first time. I try to teach Anna to recognize the pictures on my baseball cards, but she's not very good at it. I play dolly and horsey and house, and I pray no one sees me.

I used to think school days went slow, but these summer days are even slower. What was I thinking, wishing for summer? I see boys go by with fishing poles and families with picnic baskets. I think a lot about Foster and his family, hoping they are lazing the days away in Mississippi.

Most days, Mr. Weinstein plunks his paper down on the table as he heads off to work. He nods at me and says, "Gewd morrr-ning."

One time, when he first moved in, I brought his paper in off the step to read. When he came to breakfast he made a tempest in a teapot about it. Yelling at me with his funny accent, all *zees* for this and *zink* for think. "In America people have rights. You pay for this? No. I pay for this. You think I want to read my paper with little boy fingerprints here and here? No. I do not." He said all this while Mary and me tried not to laugh at all his sounds. So now I wait and read his paper after he's done with it.

Today Anna is playing dolls, but I told her I'm on strike, like the union, so I read the paper. Like my da used to, in his chair, with his tea and milk and his scone. Ma never makes scones anymore so I just have tea, with lots of milk.

I read an article about a man named W. E. B. Du Bois.

What a funny name. I wonder what all those initials stand for. He's all in a lather about the unfair treatment of blacks. He condemns lynching as barbaric blood sacrifices just for show, and I agree. What kind of people think that's a jolly time? I still have nightmares about the puppy. Yesterday at Mass, Timmy told me a black man from New Orleans got hisself killed by Ragen's Colts, right here in Chicago, for stopping in front of a pub on the west side of Wentworth Avenue.

"Don't they know better, by now?" Timmy said.

I read about President Wilson over there in France, working on a treaty. I don't understand most of it, but if Germany doesn't sign it, then we're going back to war. *For God's sake, sign the treaty,* I think.

And what about the war happening right here? What kind of a country doesn't protect its own people? Does President Wilson even know about the lynchings? Or is he so gol dang busy with his big treaty that he can't pay attention to his very own backyard? Why don't he make the South sign a treaty? No more lynchings.

If he don't do something, I ain't going to vote for him, when I'm old enough. My da and me liked Teddy Roosevelt, but he died in January, so we can't vote for him. All activity in Chicago stopped for five whole minutes the day of his funeral. Sister Salmonetti made us close our eyes and say our prayers. I still remember one thing I learned at Nativity that Roosevelt put in his writings: "Do what you can, with what you've got, where you are."

I aim to try. Unless I have to watch over Anna for the rest of my life.

I read another news story that in Washington, DC, they're doing more investigating about those dynamite bombs Emmett told us about. Attorney General Palmer's very own house got bombed, so now he's on the warpath, raiding anybody who looks the least bit suspicious, including some of those twenty-five thousand Jewish people who stormed downtown last week. They were protesting the Polish picking on the Jews in Poland. Seems like people are picking on people all over the world. I think it's the Germans that made the bombs, but Foster thinks it's the Russians.

I told Foster when school's out I was gonna investigate Mr. Weinstein, but now I find out it's me stuck watching Anna all summer. Gol dang. If I don't get it done, Mr. Palmer will beat me to it.

And here's something that's going to change our lives for sure: Congress passed the Nineteenth Amendment. It says everyone has a right to vote, even women. Ain't that something? Wonder if the women will vote Republican, like their husbands, or break off and vote for who they want? Mayor Thompson might have to start buying hats for all the ladies, come next election.

What would my da say to that? Women voting, just like men? My da was no louse to women, but I'm pretty sure he wouldn't hold with this news. He likes his supper on the table and his tea hot and ready. "Learn to make a good cup of tea, Miss High and Mighty," he used to tell Mary. "That's your lot in life."

Then I see the ad, smack dab in the center of the page, and it makes me sit up straight. My da might have a heart attack if he reads the paper. The president of the Chicago Cubs is inviting the ladies to come to Cubs Park tomorrow. Free admission. Thank the good Lord we ain't Cubs fans. Gol dang.

Timmy's da was all worked up about the idea of women voting, I remember. My last week of working on the docks, I heard him and the other dockers laughing about it.

One man said, "Last thing we need is women mucking up the elections, thinking they know as much as men."

Timmy's da put his hand to his hair and in a high voice said, "Why I do declare. He's so handsome. He has my vote." Everyone laughed.

What would my da do if he was here? Would he laugh at women voting? It's men that wears the pants in the family, he always says, so don't that mean women ain't got no reason to vote? But Ma works hard and Mary's smart, so don't that give them the right? I'm as confused as a dog with two tails. I hope my da ain't as hard-boiled stubborn as Mr. Beatty and them dockers.

And thinking about hard-boiled stubborn makes me think about Sister Salmonetti. She'll have to switch out her old Bill of Rights for a new version, won't she? It's hard to imagine Sister Salmonetti getting to vote. Maybe nuns don't vote. I bet Mary would know. Maybe I'll ask her.

When I finish reading, I dump out my teacup and throw the tea leaves in the rubbish bin. Something odd pokes up from under the eggshells and toast crusts. I fish it out, holding it to drip over the bin. It's not the *Chicago Tribune* or *The Chicago Defender*, but a torn corner of a page from a different newspaper. I can read the word STOP and another word I never heard before: POGROMS. Like programs without the R and the A. Under those two words it says, MEET AT DOUGLAS PARK, JUNE 8, and then part of a number, 000, and the word KILLED. Gol dang. It's spy stuff, for sure. They're meeting somewhere to stop something and talk about how many they've killed.

I'm more determined than ever to break into Mr. Weinstein's room. I got to find where Ma keeps the spare key.

Anna and I go outside and sit on the steps. The cottonwood trees are dropping their fluffy seeds after the rain. The seeds float around without direction, up for a while, then down. Anna chases them, twirling and giggling. I bet it's pretty down by the creek.

"Whatcha doin'?" I hear Timmy's voice and turn to see him edging up to the bottom of our steps.

Out on the street I see Mickey and some other fellows walking with their mitts. Connor is carrying a bat.

"Nothin'," I say.

Timmy motions to the street. "Come on."

"Can't." I point toward Anna, who's sitting on the ground, shaking out her shoe.

"Where's Mary?"

"At the Dolans'."

Timmy points to Anna. "Bring her with."

I run in and grab my glove, then take hold of Anna's hand.

Anna pouts. "Ma didn't say."

"Oh, come on. I'll get you an ice cream."

Anna stomps her foot, but comes along, a pout on her

face. While we tag behind the rest, Timmy tells me how he ain't been going down to the docks this week, seeing as how there's not enough work. Too many blacks, he says. And they work for cheap, because they all live together and don't have to pay mortgages. At Schaller's Pump they can't stop talking about it, he says. People are riled up. Mickey says they might go teach them blacks a lesson any day now.

It's the same old Timmy. Same old talk with a little more hate in it. Merry-go-round talk. Going nowhere. Timmy is all talk and no walk. My da hates fellows like that.

"Put your money where your mouth is," my da used to tell me when I groused about things.

Hearing Timmy blabber makes me miss Foster and the raft even more. And for the rest of the way to the ball field, my mind wanders back to the lean-to and Bubbly Creek. I want to just haul off and tell Timmy about my new best friend.

If I was down South with Foster and somebody tried any of that Jim Crow stuff, or even here in Chicago if somebody tried to teach him a lesson—well, let me at 'em. It makes me sad, not knowing when he's coming back from Mississippi. Maybe he won't ever come back.

I'm jarred out of my thinking when Mickey jabs his nose in my face.

"Are you deaf and dumb?" There's laughter. "I said you're on my team."

Mickey is a captain and the pitcher, of course. And Joey's the captain of the other team. I know most of the players. Lots of the Hamburgs. Little Frankie Ragen and Jimmie. Their das are good ballplayers from that other club down by The Stock Yard, Ragen's Colts—the one that roughs up black folks, according to the stories Emmett brings us. Also, Kevin and Connor from Nativity. And some of the fellows' little brothers, who get picked last but still dance around, just excited to be included.

Mickey and Joey choose which team bats first by alternating hands down the length of the bat—first Mickey's hand, then Joey's, until Joey is the last to fit his whole hand before the knob.

I park Anna way behind halfway between the backstop and the street and point my finger at her. "Don't wander off."

"I'm thirsty," she says.

"Here." I pull a piece of a broken sweet stick from my pocket, rip the wrapper down, pick off the lint from the top, and hand it to her.

It feels like such a long walk just to get to the edge of the field. And I can't even see the street behind the outfield fence.

Boy, hitting a home run here would really be something. Not like at the empty lot where Foster and me play, home run balls rolling down the alley. The high school, De La Salle, uses this field and there's an actual dirt diamond and a bench for the players to sit on. The outfield gets mowed regularly. I bet it costs a pretty penny to go here for high school.

Mickey walks over to me. "Watching your kid sister, huh? Whaddaya play?"

I shrug. "I play third, sometimes."

"Okay, take third," he says, and points each of his players to a position. All the little brothers skedaddle off to the outfield, whooping and hollering. I check on Anna before I head to third base.

"I wanna go home," she whines. Her mouth is sticky and purple.

"In a bit." I pick a dandelion and put it in her lap. "Here."

"Get out here, Daideo," Mickey yells from the pitcher's mound, and the players on the bench laugh 'cause Daideo is what some kids call their granddas.

I run onto the field, and right away I'm no longer William Jarlath McDermott. I'm the Ginger Kid, Buck Weaver, third baseman for the Chicago White Sox. I own third base. I dance around it. I sway. I yell, "Hey, batter, batter. Swing."

Mickey and his Hamburg Athletic Club boys are good. They play on league teams at night, just like Ragen's Colts do. Really, the rest of us are just here to run after foul balls and chase down home runs. I don't make any plays on third. A pop-up to Mickey and two out at first. I have to admit, Mickey is a good pitcher.

Then we're up to bat. I'm ready to show off. I know Timmy and I are strong from working on the docks, and when I get up to bat I find out I'm stronger than I even knew. I crank a good one all the way to the edge of the outfield—but one of the little brothers catches it with a stroke of luck, and I'm out, still smug with how far I hit the ball.

Mickey sits down on the bench next to me, a piece of grass between his teeth. I smell his sweat and the soap smell of Mennen's Shaving Cream. It feels nice to be at the field, with other fellows. Lazy like. And it's quiet for a bit while we wait for Joey's outfielders to get to their positions.

Our first batter heads to the plate and Mickey leans his shoulder into mine. "Where's your sister?"

I point to Anna, who's still picking dandelions behind the backstop.

"Not her. Your other sister."

"Mary? Working."

"Where at?"

"Dolans'." The Dolans run the café where Ma works. Whenever we bellyache about how rich they are, Ma always says, "The good Lord blesses whom he chooses. And Gracie Dolan has been a blessing to me." The Dolans have something to do with The Union Stock Yard. They go on vacation for a whole week in the summer, and not just to visit relatives. They have a car of their own. And season tickets for White Sox games. One time they even give me and Da their seats, right up close to the batter's box. That's when Da caught Buck Weaver's foul ball. While the rest of us are scraping by, they do okay.

"She's pretty," says Mickey.

"Yah. Ma says Mrs. Dolan is blessed." Ma is always talking about Mrs. Dolan. Her hair. Her shoes.

Mickey laughs. "Mary, I mean."

I don't know what to say to that. Does Mickey know about Mary's shadow, Joey? Does Mickey want to be Mary's fellow, too? Ma won't approve, for sure. But I can't see how Mary would ever fancy Mickey, with his bossy ways. They'd fight like those Kilkenny cats from the Irish story, until only their tails were left. Or maybe Mickey's just making conversation and don't mean anything special about Mary. Still, I'm glad when Timmy strikes out at the plate so we can head back out to the field.

I feel good about chumming it up with Mickey. Maybe the episode with the puppy happened because he was drinking. Maybe Ma is wrong about the Hamburgs. Maybe we can all live under the shelter of each other and survive. Maybe someday both Timmy and I will be official Hamburg boys.

I take third base seriously. Two outs to first. A couple of hits. There's a runner on second and third. And now the ball is skidding straight down the third base line and I'm on it. It hits my glove. I step on third, then whip it to the catcher. Double play. Oh yeah! Take that, Ginger Kid. In a few years I'll take your spot on the White Sox. I jog to the bench, all puffed up with pride.

Mickey claps me on the shoulder. "Good play, Billy, but there were already three outs when you tagged third."

"Oh, yah. That's right," I say, and I feel right silly.

"You know them Dolans pay the bleedin' scabs to cross the picket line, don't you?"

I shake my head. "I don't know nothing about that."

Mickey's hand is still on my shoulder. "So, is Mary at the Dolans' right now?"

"I think so." I don't like the way his hand is squeezing my shoulder. I don't like his face so close to mine. And

I don't like the way he raises his eyebrows when he says Mary's name.

I shrug off his hand and walk over to behind the backstop to check on Anna. I know I'm in trouble when I see her dress. Mud everywhere—and her face matches. "Whaddaya doing?" I cry.

"Making a cake," she says, patting a pile of mud in front of her. "I want to get ice cream."

"Okay, almost." One more turn at bat, then I better get her home.

Mickey meets me on my way back to the bench. "Tell me about your friend, Billy."

"What friend?"

"The one who lives by the river."

My heart gets very still. Punched into silence by the fear fist.

I stammer. "He—he ain't my friend. Just a kid in my class. He—he don't live by the river. He just showed me his fort. That's all."

My eyes scan the field and I see Timmy. His blue shirt and his black cap. He's staring at me.

The no-good traitor! It *was* him spying on us at the creek. I'll kill him.

"What's his name, Billy?" Mickey prods.

"Why do you want to know?" I ask quiet and quick, then worry for talking back to Mickey. I clench my teeth and back up to make a grab for Anna.

"Does Mary know his name, Billy?" Mickey moves toward me.

"No!" I shout. "He's just a kid in my class."

"I might have to go ask Mary. She might know."

"Leave her alone."

"How many are there, Billy? What are their names?"

"I don't know."

"Mary might be late home tonight."

I pull on Anna's hand. It's warm and sticky.

There's a shift in the breeze. A waft of stockyard stink hits my nose. It smells like the waste of death. I need my da.

"They ain't nobody, just brothers making a fort. They're on vacation now, anyway."

"That's right, Billy. Just brothers, living in a fort. Stealing our property. Stealing our jobs. Taking our bleedin' money to go on vacation. There's going to be hell to pay. There's going to be trouble."

Mickey's next to me now. He puts his arm around the top of my shoulders, then moves it to my neck. He squeezes and I can't breathe. *This is what a lynching feels like*, I think.

"You know what, Billy? Tell me their names and I'll try to protect them."

I can't think straight. I don't know what to do. Mary, my sister. Foster, my best friend. Mickey, my neighborhood watchdog. He won't hurt any of us, will he?

"Williams. Foster and Odell. And Emmett. They don't live in a fort and they don't steal. I barely know them. They live with their auntie, past Wentworth." I choke it out, my voice high and babyish.

Then I walk away fast, tugging Anna to keep up. The air is full of cottonwood seeds now. They have no destination, no direction. Caught up by the least little turmoil and blown off course.

They're cowards, like me.

Chapter Nine

"WHERE'S MY ICE CREAM?" ANNA pulls against my hand, her feet planted on the street. "I want ice cream!" Saints have mercy, but she's a strong four-year-old. She's screaming now and mothers on the sidewalk are looking at me.

I dig my fingernails into her wrists and say, through gritted teeth, "Shut up or I'll leave you here."

And then she sobs. Big, heaving sobs with no breath in between. "I'm sorry, Billy. Don't leave me here. Don't leave me."

Doggone it. I feel terrible. I'm a double-crossing best

friend and a lousy brother. I don't know what to do. And it's hard to think with Anna crying.

Mickey won't hurt Mary, will he? I could tell on him. But that might be throwing a rock at a hornet's nest. I could snitch on Mary and her sneaking around with Joey. Then Ma would keep a close eye on Mary. But what if Mickey talks to Mary about me going to the creek? If Mary tells on me we'll both be done for.

There I go again. Worrying about me, myself, and I, instead of my best friend.

Timmy's joke again.

Mickey and his boys won't be able to find the Williams's house because I spilled my guts, will they? Near as I can figure, they live on South State Street, past what's called The Stroll, because people always slow down when they pass, listening to the jazz music from the clubs around there. Somewhere in the Black Belt. But they're in Mississippi for the summer, ain't they? Or out working, not hanging at the fort in the middle of the day.

Then a little tickle reminds me that Timmy said the docks were slow. Foster might be at the fort, hoping I show up. He might be watching for me, his double-crossing blood brother.

"Problems, Billy?" I hear a deep voice and squint up to

see the shiny badge and silver buttons of Officer O'Brien. He stoops and pats Anna on the head. He lives on our block and goes to Nativity. He and my da left on the same day for the war, but he come back with just a limp, not shell shock. Officer O'Brien's round belly bulges out under his long jacket and I can see his billy club hanging off his belt.

"Nah. No problems. She just wants some ice cream." Would Officer O'Brien help me? One time he fixed the railing on our stairs. He's always on patrol in Bridgeport. But I worry he's a friend to the Hamburgs. He might play cards with them at Schaller's, or even help out with their baseball leagues. He might be a one of Mayor Thompson's patsies.

Officer O'Brien picks Anna up. "Little lady, you sure are making a fuss. Let's get you some ice cream."

Anna sticks her tongue out at me and beams at him. He gives me a wink, his eyes very blue in his ruddy face, and sets out. I tag along, feeling again like the cottonwood seed, and wishing for my da to tell me what to do, to be a shoulder to me. Officer O'Brien pushes open the door of Woolworth Five and Dime, walks in, and plops Anna down on a stool.

The waitress takes our order and brings our ice cream, and my sister, the little faker, smiles and smiles, everyone cooing over how cute she is.

"Billy, look. It's got creamy and a cherry." She pokes her tongue into the whipping cream.

"Use your spoon," I say.

Officer O'Brien sets his hat down on the stool next to him and wipes his sweaty brow. I keep my glove in my lap. We talk about the White Sox. They're playing at home today after eighteen games on the road.

"They lost eleven bleedin' games, Billy. Eleven, by God."

"Yep, those Tigers whooped them good. They lost the whole bleedin' series," I say, spicing up my language when I'm talking man-to-man with Officer O'Brien, even though Ma don't allow it.

My mouth is yammering about baseball but my head is worrying about Foster. I'm in such a state I can't sit still. I keep fiddling with the laces on my glove.

"Those White Sox got you all upset, don't they?" Officer O'Brien notices. "Gotta win these three against the Indians. Then they're off again. Maybe we'll catch a game, whaddaya say, Billy?"

"Yeah, sure." But I know it won't happen. Can't happen, really. With me watching Anna and him coaching and working. I feel that little empty spot under my ribs get a little more hollow, wishing me and my da could go to a game together.

"Billy," Officer O'Brien says when we finish and go our separate ways. "You best keep away from the docks. You hear me? There's trouble brewing. You stick to the neighborhood. Be a good soldier for your da." He raises his eyebrows and nods his head in the direction of the creek. The he sets his hat on his head, straightens his jacket over his round belly, and waves at Anna. "See you in church, Billy."

How does he know about the creek? I'm glad I didn't tell Officer O'Brien what Mickey said.

When me and Anna climb the steps to our flat, Ma opens the door so fast I tumble inside, my fist on the doorknob.

"William Jarlath McDermott, where have you been?"

Anna says, "Sir Callan bought me ice cream. Billy, too."

"Officer O'Brien," I explain. "She made a fuss."

"Billy promised."

Ma's gaze lands on Anna. "Bless my sore eyes. Little Missy, aren't you a sight? Go clean her up, Billy."

"Ma, can I go see Timmy? Please?"

"I have a shift at five. And this washing is ready to hang." Her shoulders droop down, but she never complains. Not my ma.

"Please, Ma."

"Oh, all right. Go on then. I'll take care of Little Missy." And she gives me a quick peck on my cheek.

"Don't worry, Ma. I'll get it done," I say. And I run. Fast.

First I check on Mary. She's sitting on the porch swing with one of the Dolan girls. I wave and she waves back.

Then I take off for Bubbly Creek. I cut through vacant lots and get chased by two dogs. I stop and hide behind a fence and watch the street. I'm a ball of nerves. That fear fist is banging me up inside. I say the Our Father and whisper a plea that Foster will be at the lean-to so I can talk to him, or in Mississippi so nothing bad can happen to him. I don't care which.

Once I find the creek, I head north. It's overgrown on the banks so I take off my shoes and walk along the cement wall that edges the water. I see some washing hung on a line between the trees, and low spots where campfires have burned out. I see the canvas roof of a tent, barely visible in the branches. It makes me wonder about what Mickey said, about people living by the creek. Stealing our property.

I hear the camp by the river before I see it. The rattle of the stones as the water rushes over them. Bubbling. Babbling. So familiar, my home away from home. Nothing can happen. I can't lose this place, these friends.

I call out when I see Foster sitting on our rock by the

creek. He jumps and looks at me, then hops off the rock and runs toward me. But he doesn't smile.

"Billy, whatcha doing here?"

"You're back from Mississippi?"

"You gotta go, Billy."

"Why? What's wrong?"

Foster looks down, rolls his toes over a dead branch.

"What? What is it?" Maybe he already knows I betrayed him. Maybe he feels my shame seeping out of me.

He glances at the lean-to, and I notice the flimsy pallet doors we rigged up are pulled closed. "My daddy's sleeping."

"But . . ."

"I knew you didn't know. Odell said you did. But I knew you thought we was just playing here, not living here." His toes keep rolling the branch. Back and forth. Back and forth. "It's just, we're sending money to my mama while we save up for a place." Back and forth.

"When we first come, we was with my auntie, but it was so crowded. All three of us in the same bed. Only one toilet." The branch breaks apart, crumbling under Foster's toes. "Have you seen where black folks live? The Black Belt? People all jumbled together like ants? So we're staying here, until it gets cold."

I ain't seen. But I heard. I heard it's worse than The

Stock Yard. Stink and all. "But you ain't allowed to camp on public property. There's laws, ain't there?"

"Nah. Squatter's rights, my daddy says."

Just then the lean-to doors move. Two brown feet poke out, followed by the long body of Foster's father. I don't want to stare but I can't stop myself. I see a tall man, with a lean face, not round like Foster's. Foster's daddy looks like a grown-up Odell, their faces long with deep-set, wide, knowing eyes under high foreheads.

I feel stupid thinking the lean-to was just our fort. And sore at Foster for not telling me it wasn't. We were the same. Me with two sisters. Him with two brothers. Me with just a ma and him with just a daddy. But we're different now. I have a home. A real home. And he lives in the woods, stealing from everybody, just like Mickey says.

Foster pulls me back into the brush. He whispers, "Go, Billy. Just go."

"Why?" Why does he want me to go? Why didn't he tell me the truth? Why do people have to live like this?

"'Cause he works second shift at the Pick Factory."

"No, I mean why don't you want him to see me?"

Foster says nothing. We both swat at mosquitos buzzing in our ears. The creek bubbles on and we watch Foster's dad stir up the fire and put a coffeepot over the coals, his back to us. Finally, in a low and quiet voice Foster says, "You know how it is at school? How we can't always be friends? Well, it goes both ways."

"But I'm not like that. You know that." *But aren't you a little like that?* whispers a voice in my ear. *Not choosing a side?*

"Not you. Him." And Foster nods his head toward his daddy.

The realization smacks me upside my head. His daddy might hate me because I'm white. I remember now, when Odell said, *I don't hate white people,* as though he knew people who did. It's a whole different feeling when the paint is on the other side of the fence, ain't it?

And to think this is how it is for Foster. All the time. Everywhere he goes. It's not just a few people for him, but most of Chicago. How can he just put his eyes down? How can he stop the fighting feeling?

"Fozzy. Where you at?" his daddy calls.

Foster pushes my shoulder and mouths, "Go." Then he steps silently out of the woods and walks toward the campfire.

I'm quiet, too, as I head the other direction. Am I different in my thinking because of my da? What would he say now that I'm blacklisted by my best friend's daddy?

I'm about a hundred feet away when I remember Mickey's words. *There's going to be hell to pay. There's going to be trouble.*

I think about the puppy. I think about my sister Mary. How it's my fault if she gets hurt. I think about how I betrayed Foster, my best friend. I want to run far away, jump in a hole, hide forever.

Is this what happened to my da? Is this shell shock? Maybe he wasn't chicken, but just got confused. Too many choices. Not knowing what to do. God Almighty. What kind of soldier will I be? What's the point of going off to war to fight for right, if I don't even know what's right anymore?

But I do know how to make things right, don't I? Because he taught me, didn't he now? My da taught me. *To stand up for what's right, you have to cross the line.* He told me not to be a coward. I'm beginning to understand now. My da helped that black man out, and he got punched in the eye for it. It ain't free if I want to be friends with Foster and his brothers. There's costs to be paid.

I turn around and stomp back to the creek. The branches bite at my legs, and the mosquitos tease me, but can't land on my sweaty face. Both Foster and his daddy stare at me in wonder.

I stick out my hand. "I'm Billy. I'm Foster's friend from school. His best friend." I squint my eyes at Foster, daring him to stop me.

Mr. Williams wipes his hand on his overalls and shakes mine, his huge, brown, calloused hand completely covering my small, white one.

"Welcome, Billy. Will you sit a spell?" His voice is low and slow, like Odell's, but his words are even longer. "Spayal" for spell. He hands me a square of cotton to wipe away my sweat.

"He just come, Daddy. I didn't ask him to come." Foster's eyes are popping out of his face and I roll mine at him.

So what, my eyes say.

"Fozzy. We ain't got much. But we do got manners." He strokes his chin. "So this here's Billy who helping you with that raft? Billy from the South Side?" Foster's daddy's eyebrows raise up high on his forehead.

And it's clear, clear as day, from the baffled look on Mr. Williams's face that I'm not who he expected. And it's clear from the dismayed look on Foster's face that he left out the little part about me being a white Irish boy from Bridgeport.

I know my face is beet red. Not just from the hot, hot afternoon, but from being embarrassed at Foster lying to his daddy about me. But I won't let my shell shock get the best of me. "Mr. Williams. I'm sorry to bother you, sir, but I came here to tell you something, and I aim to spit it out."

Then I just let the words tumble out of me. Everything Mickey said and did. And Officer O'Brien, too.

When I finish, Mr. Williams goes to the lean-to and brings back a metal box. He hands me some newspaper clippings.

The first one is an article by that man Du Bois, from a page ripped out of a magazine called *The Crisis,* which I never heard of. Mr. Williams points out a section under-lined with a pencil:

We return.
We return from fighting.
We return fighting.
Make way for Democracy! We saved it in France,
and by the Great Jehovah, we will save it in the
United States of America, or know the reason why.

The next article is from *The Chicago Defender,* the newspa-per Foster and I buy, mine hidden under my mattress. It's by James Johnson. The word "lynching" jumps out at me and I read the underlined words:

I ask not only black Americans but white Americans,
are you not ashamed of lynching? . . . The nation is
today striving to lead the moral forces of the world
in the support of the weak against the strong; well,
I'll tell you it can't do it until it conquers and crushes
out this monster in its own midst.

The air is still and sticky. The buzzing and clicking of the insects in the woods never stops. I wish for a sliver of cool ice to rub all over my face. I pick up one more clipping, by Du Bois again. I read the underlined parts again.

One ever feels his two-ness, an American, a Negro;
two souls, two thoughts, two unreconciled strivings;
two warring ideals in one dark body, whose dogged
strength alone keeps it from being torn asunder. The
history of the American Negro is the history of this
strife . . . He simply wishes to make it possible for a
man to be both a Negro and an American without
being cursed and spit upon by his fellows, without
having the doors of opportunity closed roughly in
his face.

Mr. Williams fishes down to the bottom of the box and

pulls out a magazine with a red cover and a drawing of two women carrying a basket. It's called *The Liberator*. Twenty cents. He turns to the middle and points to a poem by Claude McKay. I read it and my heart starts to pound. Not just from fear of what the poem means, but with a thrill that finally, black people are going to fight back. Oh, Mickey is right, for sure. There will be hell to pay, but this time, black people ain't going to be the only ones that pay.

I close the magazine. Mr. Williams raises his eyes to the trees and his deep voice echoes in the woods.

If we must die, let it not be like hogs . . .
So that our precious blood may not be shed
In vain; then even the monsters we defy
Shall be constrained to honor us though dead!
Like men we'll face the murderous, cowardly pack,
Pressed to the wall, dying, but fighting back!

Foster stands close to me, our arms touching. We have no words to say. We can't pretend the world works the way we want it to any longer.

Mr. Williams says, "W. E. B. Du Bois came to Mississippi. He spoke at a gathering in our church, talked about saving our black bodies and your white souls." He pokes at the fire and touches the side of the coffeepot with a quick finger to see if it's ready. "I do believe trouble will come, Billy, and when it do, my body will thank your soul for the warning."

"I'm sorry. I'm not . . . I mean, my da . . ." I don't know how to say we don't hate black people. That I don't hate black people. That even though it might be too late, I ain't going to be a coward. "You know we're not like—"

Mr. Williams interrupts me in his slow and steady way. "Son. We all do what we can, with what we have, where we are."

"Teddy Roosevelt said that," I say, proud of myself.

Mr. Williams smiles a sad smile and drops the articles back into the metal box. "Some would say President Wilson isn't doing all he can, with what he has, where he is, to help stop the monster and open up the doors of opportunity. It's hard to know the best course of action. But I always believed what my mama taught me: 'Do justly, love mercy, and walk humbly with thy God.'"

"That's from the Good Book," Foster says.

Just then the raindrops start to fall and I know I got to go. Ma's waiting on me to watch Anna during her evening shift, and she'll be mad as a wet hen if I don't do something with the washing, at least put it some of it on the fold-up clothes dryer until the sun comes out tomorrow.

Mr. Williams shakes my hand, and ruffles up my hair the way my da used to. "Don't you worry now, son. We can take care of ourselves. A friend of Foster's is a friend of mine, even if he do come from the South Side." He winks at me.

I head up the path that goes to the docks, instead of through the woods the way I come, thinking about Mr. Williams. How bad it must've been in Mississippi to make him run away to Chicago to risk living in a lean-to. If it gets bad here in Chicago will they keep running? Me and Foster could go first and scout out a place. Take the raft as far as she'll go, then hitch a ride. Send word to the others when it's safe. When the water's deep enough to cover those rocks of hate again.

Just as I climb the bank to the street I see Odell and Emmett coming from work, but I turn the other way and run, hoping they don't see me, hoping they won't know what a traitor I been. Hoping Foster and his daddy keep my warning a secret.

Chapter Ten

BEFORE I KNOW IT JULY 4th comes. Ma makes a picnic and we take the trolley to Sixty-Third Street Beach, not our usual beach. A brand-new bathing pavilion just got built and Ma wants to see it. Along Garfield Boulevard I see signs pounded into the trees: NEGROES GO HOME. WE WILL GET YOU. What a lousy thing to do on a holiday.

Mary sure acts strange. She walks weird, like a peacock, sticking out her chest with her chin up in the air, and she sits all prim and proper on her towel. Me and Anna play in the sand and the water, but when I dump a bucket on Mary, Ma gets mad at me. Then Ma gets mad at Mary 'cause she walks to the pavilion without her cover-up on. Boys whistle. Gol dang. Girls are weird.

We eat our picnic and drink our sodas, a special treat Ma brought from the diner. Everybody is supposed to be drinking sodas and nothing else, now that they have wartime prohibition, but I still see plenty of folks with bottles that ain't soda. All Chicago went crazy the night before the law started on July 1. The paper said folks spent two million dollars buying liquor.

Ma says the diner and the grocer been selling out of raisin cakes, on account of how the raisins can go belly-up and ferment into wine. I asked Ma what will happen to Mr. Beatty and his love of the poison, and she said there's plenty of doctors that applied for special licenses just for that problem. I sure hope they help Mr. Beatty—for Timmy and his ma's sake.

As we're sitting there, I notice all around me are white people, no blacks. I notice these things, these days. After Foster's daddy and the newspaper articles. I watch for these things on the street and in the paper. They say the North is the new South, the flood of Southerners bringing the race problems to Chicago when they come.

But I don't think so. I think the race problem is like a sliver. Once you got it in you, it just takes a little irritation to make it dig in deeper and fester. And it seems a whole lot of people in Chicago just realized they been having slivers in them for their whole life.

We sit together on the blanket and watch the fireworks reflected in Lake Michigan. The booms echo off the buildings. Do they let shell-shocked soldiers watch the fireworks? What is my da thinking? Can he remember good stuff, or only bad? Does he remember fireworks with me and Mary? Or only war and death?

I won't let him go to war again. Instead, I will go. And nobody will stop me.

I lean over so Ma can hear me. "You don't got to worry about Da going back to war. I'm going to join up in the Field Artillery."

"There aren't going to be any more wars. They signed that treaty a week ago," Ma says.

I forgot about that. Finally President Wilson got it done. The Treaty of Versailles. "Well, just in case, you don't got to worry," I tell her again.

"That's a mighty nice blessing, Billy, but you do have a few years yet. In the meantime, can I count on you to be a good soldier at home?" She pats my hand.

"Aw, sure, Ma." I lean back and think how fine it is to let your ma know she can count on you.

"They're releasing Da from the hospital," she says, "and I'll need your help."

I sit up fast. "But he can't walk or talk or nothing," I bellow.

"That's right, Billy. So it'll be you that keeps an eye on him while I'm off to the diner."

I can't believe it. I said I'd be a soldier, not a nurse. How's he going to get up the stairs? Get into bed? Go to the privy? "What about Mary? Why do I always get stuck at home?" Gol dang. It's bad enough I'm watching over Anna all the time. Now Da, too?

Ma hisses at me. "What a shameful thing to say, Billy. Your da worked his whole life for us. Mary works hard all day at the Dolans'. And she's studying for that correspondence course at night. What do you need to do that's more important than your da, for the love of God?"

So it's me that has the double duty, nursemaiding all day *and* night. One of these days I'm going to bust out. I'm almost old enough. Then somebody else can be on house duty and see how they like it.

We pack up and walk away from the lake. It's still hotter than hot. When we get home we listen to the rebroadcast of the big fight on the radio. Jack Dempsey and the heavyweight champ Jess Willard. In Toledo, Ohio. The announcer says it's 110 degrees in the ring. It might be 110 degrees in our front room, too. I get out the map to look up Toledo, Ohio. Someday, I will buy me a car. I will drive to see fights all over the country. Even go to Jackson, Mississippi, to visit Foster's family. I'm his best friend from up North, I'll tell them. I'm the one who warned him trouble might be coming. I'm the one who crossed the line for him.

But just then a little voice whispers in my ear. *You ain't done nothing. All you done was get a few mosquito bites and tell them something they already knew.*

Da comes home in an ambulance five days later, and the orderlies muscle him up the steps. He doesn't talk. Just stares and smiles. Ma pushes his wheelchair from the bedroom to the front room every day. Anna crawls up on his lap and he pats her head. Mary makes him a cup of tea and flounces out the door to her important job. I watch Da dribble his tea all down his shirt and it makes me sick.

Timmy comes by the next day, bringing a pot of stew and a loaf of bread.

"Well, bless your Ma, Timmy. Give her our thanks for thinking of us," says Ma.

I walk Timmy to the door.

"Tough break," he says.

"Sure is. But he's getting better. Good as new soon, I think."

Timmy doesn't look convinced. "Think you'll ever be able to come by again?" he asks. "Go to the docks? Play some ball?" Timmy's acting just how I feel. Like life is over for me. As if there's no more tomorrows.

"Sure. Sure I can. Next chance I get," I lie. Next chance I get, I aim to head to the creek.

After Timmy leaves I do my own stewing. Is Da really getting better? Will he ever be good as new? Ain't life just upside down and backwards, me taking care of the one who's supposed to take care of me? I sure hope he gets better. Or his life is over, and ours, too. I know the army sends money to Ma, but it don't make up for what happened to my da.

One day a week or so later, Ma comes home and says the diner closed early on account of the fuse box blowing. "It's too hot. We can't keep ice in the icebox and the fans running." She lifts her skirt and billows it to cool off. "Billy, shoo," she says to me. "Smells like rain. Go play before the storm."

And I'm off like a loose rat to Timmy's house. It's a struggle not to go to the creek, but I dropped Anna with

Mary at the Dolans' just yesterday so I could go work on the raft, and I don't want to wear out my welcome in the lean-to or my favors with Mary. And I do feel bad I ain't been to see Timmy since he stopped by.

"You going to the docks today?" I ask when I see him sitting on his porch.

He whoops. "Race you there!" And he takes off.

We reach the factory where they're doing the construction just as the first drops of rain plop on our heads. Timmy ducks under the barricade and around the corner into the factory.

"Come on," he yells.

I don't want to get in trouble for trespassing, but the workers are all gone on account of the rain. I follow Timmy up a stairway and then up a ladder and just like that, we're on the third floor of the factory. It ain't too safe, with some floorboards missing and bricks piled up near the open windows. They must be redoing the casements around the window, and the damp wind whistles right through. The cars and buggies going by on Thirty-Fifth Street look mighty small from up here.

Timmy picks up a brick from the pile. "There's that no-good fruit wagon. Stealing business from the white folks' grocery store."

I recognize the wagon. It's Montgomery & Son's Produce. Mr. Montgomery is a real nice black man. He comes down to the docks for his crates of fruit and vegetables and always tosses us an apple or something. When Ma has a little extra cash she buys from him.

Timmy hauls off and throws the brick, and it hits the horse's rump. The horse rears up and Mr. Montgomery falls backwards, just catching himself before he tips into the wagon. The horse takes off down the street with Mr. Montgomery struggling to get his balance and grab hold of the reins. As they bump over the cobblestones, fruit bounces out of the wagon.

Timmy laughs. "Did you see that? I hit that horse square on the bum." He hands me a brick. "Take a turn." He points at a garbage wagon driven by a couple of black men. "Did you hear about them terror cars in Washington, DC? Blacks shooting from a car window, killing people going to the Naval Hospital?"

When I hesitate, he grabs another brick. "Come on. What're you waiting for?" He launches the brick at the garbage wagon, but it misses and hits the street, shattering into dust. He throws another and laughs like a maniac. "Look at us. We're a terror factory."

Two ladies walking by tilt their umbrellas and look

up so they can see where the rocks are coming from. One points at the third-floor window of the factory, where we're standing.

I want to clear out of there. "Your da will skin you alive if he catches you in here. Come on." I move to the ladder and head down.

"You ain't nothing but a yellow-bellied sissy," Timmy says and I don't answer. Maybe I am. And maybe it's just a little prank, but it feels like more. It feels like we think we own the world and they got to pay to live in it. Just like Mickey hurt that puppy for being in the street, and that boy charged Foster a sandwich to go to the docks. And like the officers who warned Foster to keep off the bridge. Making people pay when it's free for everybody else.

The dock work goes slow the rest of the day. I don't say much to Timmy. I'm about to pick up my second load from one of the regulars when I see a black man waiting for work. I motion for him to take a turn with this next load and move off the dock to wait on the street for the next barge.

Timmy comes running over. "What's ailing you? You hurt or something?"

"Nah," I say. "Just taking a break."

"A break from what? You only moved one load. You're helping them out."

"Thank you kindly," the man says when he returns for the rest of the load. "This rain don't help me feed my children."

Timmy grits his teeth and walks away, and when the barges silently slip down the river and the gray of the water and the sky blend together, we both go home without saying another word.

On the way home, thinking about that man and his children, I decide to make a promise to myself. A promise I will keep. Not like Big Bill Thompson, promising black folks good jobs and safe homes and going back on his word. There's something I want to do and I aim to do it. I'll pick the perfect day. My da and Foster will be so happy. When I slip into bed I say my prayers for Da and the Williams brothers, and that God will help me keep my promises. When I fall asleep, I dream I own a ship named the *Promise Keeper* and I give free rides around the world to all my friends and family.

Chapter Eleven

ON THE MORNING OF JULY 25th I wake up sweating. Another scorcher. I read in the paper it's the hottest summer on record. But it's not only the weather that's hot.

The country's gone wild with rioting. Texas. Arizona. And in our very own capitol of Washington, DC. White people, some in uniform, hunt down black people, and when the police refuse to help, black people get mad and take matters into their own hands. "The killing was only stopped," the newspaper says, "by a merciful downpour of rain."

I find the sports section. The White Sox play St. Louis

today and I remember my promise to myself. Yep. Today is the day. It's a great thing I aim to do.

Little by little my da's been getting better. He can walk between the wheelchair and the sofa. He can use a fork and a spoon. He can point when he needs something, and when I read him the baseball scores, he raises his fist for a White Sox win.

I been earning nothing, watching him and Anna all day, but in my Wise Pig bank I saved enough pennies for this great, but maybe terrible thing. My Wise Pig holds a sign that says, SAVE A PENNY YESTERDAY, ANOTHER SAVE TODAY, TOMORROW SAVE ANOTHER, TO KEEP THE WOLF AWAY. I do need to be prepared for when the wolf comes knocking on my door, but right now my White Sox need their biggest fan, so I shake my few coins right out of the Wise Pig.

I know in my heart it's a good idea, but my head is nagging that it might be a bad idea, and get me into trouble. But whenever I had a hard time choosing at the candy store, my da always used to tell me, "Make up your mind, Billy. Your heart knows your mind."

And so I make up my mind and follow my heart. Today's the day I keep that promise I made to myself.

I watch the clock. If we're going to make it, I have to start preparing to leave just after lunch. Ma and Mary won't be home till after five. First thing I do is walk Anna over to the Dolans'. I haven't used up too many favors with Mary yet. I tell Mary just to bring Anna home with her if I'm not back from playing baseball at De La Salle field.

"Billy. Not all day."

"It's baseball, Mary. No telling how long." I shrug.

Then I run all the way to Bubbly Creek. I slow down when I get close to the lean-to. Foster is poking around in the fire pit and he's alone, barefoot and bare-chested. I throw a little rock near the fire and he jumps, then sees me and smiles.

"Come on." I motion to him. "Your long-lost relative is pitching today."

"Huh?"

"Williams. Lefty Williams. He's pitching for the Sox today."

Foster runs back to the lean-to and comes out with his shoes on. He hurries toward me, buttoning his white long-sleeved shirt. I explain what we're going to do while we scurry down the path.

And he explains back: he can't go.

"Why not?" I want to know. "I'll pay."

"You'll see," he says. "Ain't no way they'll let me in. Only white folks go to White Sox baseball games. We should go to a Giants game."

"Huh?"

"You know, the Chicago American Giants, Rube Foster's team. The one I told you about. They're going to be in the NNL next year. They're the champs."

"Nah," I say. "You're wrong. You're the one who'll see."

When we get to my house, I tell him to wait at the bottom of the stairs while I run up. Before I dragged Anna off to the Dolans' to be Mary's burden for the day, I put Da's good shirt and tie on his lap. He's managed to get his shirt on, but not buttoned. I quick do it up and throw the tie around his neck in a hasty knot, plop his hat on his head, and help him up.

Slowly. One foot, then two, on each step until we finally make it to the bottom. Foster comes out from under the stairs and I introduce him to my da. My da shakes his hand, man-to-man, just like I knew he would, and a little spark of happiness tickles my heart.

I run back up for the wheelchair while Foster keeps an eye on Da sitting on the bottom step. And then we're off. It's a glorious day for a ball game. The St. Louis Browns have a good record. Fifty-five to twenty-nine. But the White Sox been playing stellar.

There's a bundle of people heading to the game, all in their Sunday best. I'm glad I thought to get Da dressed proper. We head up Union and turn right on Thirty-Fifth.

"My da used to take me to games this way. Looks different, though," I tell Foster. *Looks different*, I think, *now that I'm the one taking* him.

Foster doesn't say much, which is unusual. He has his hands in his pockets and shuffles his feet.

"What's wrong?"

"Nothin'."

"Here, take a turn," I say, and step out from behind Da's wheelchair.

It's slow going with the chair, heaving it up and down the sidewalk curbs and paying attention to stay out of people's way. I'm glad we left plenty early.

I dance alongside the wheelchair while Foster takes a turn pushing. "White Sox, Da! White Sox!"

Da grins at me and raises his fist.

I go through the White Sox lineup for Foster. "Lefty Williams is the pitcher. We won't see Eddie Cicotte, 'cause he's not pitching. Well, maybe we will, if Williams goes wild. Schalk's the catcher. Did you know the tavern owner's wife, Ma McCuddy, feeds him on account of he's so skinny and Mr. Comiskey himself told her to?"

We're so close I can see the baseball palace of the world. Mr. Comiskey knows how to build a ballpark, that's for sure.

"Maybe Shoeless Joe will hit a homer. We'll catch it, won't we? He's hitting over three hundred. And Happy Felsch, he'll get a run for sure. They're going for the series again. Like two years ago, against New York."

We cross the railroad tracks and Da holds onto his armrests as he knocks against the sides of the wheelchair. Beads of sweat run down his nose and his face is tomato red.

A freight car is pulled off the main track, and the door is open. A man with big pincher tongs loads ice into sacks and boxes for the people in line to buy it. I motion for Foster to push Da closer while I get in line. I explain to the people in line that I just want a sliver for my da, and they push me forward so it's not long until I'm in front of the boxcar door.

"Where's your sack, sonny?"

"Can I just buy a sliver? For my da?" I point to the wheelchair. Foster is fanning my da's face with his cap.

"Wounded in the Great War?"

I nod.

"Same here," the man says, and he points to his missing leg. His pants leg is folded above the knee, and he's balancing on a crutch. For the thousandth time I wish my da only lost his leg and not his memory. And for the thousandth time I get that guilty, clanging feeling in my chest for wishing it.

"Here you go, son." The man gives me a huge chunk of ice wrapped in a newspaper. "No charge. Going to the game?"

"Yes, sir," I say. "Thanks. Thanks a lot. And I'm sorry about your leg."

Foster takes out his pocketknife and we take turns chipping away at the chunk until there's a piece for each of us and one for Da. I rub his face with the ice and then put it in his hand and show him how to put it in his mouth.

Foster still hasn't said a word.

"You okay?" I ask him. Maybe he's not used to this heat.

"Did you notice the line for ice, Billy?" he says, in a tight, quiet voice.

I shake my head, my mouth clamped tight shut on my sliver.

"Mostly black folks."

I turn around. He's right. I did sort of notice, I guess. "So?"

"So, white folks got ice boxes. Black folks got to stand in line for ice."

Lately Foster says these things. Whites have better beaches. Whites have better playgrounds. Whites have better jobs. And I know it. I didn't see it before, but I'm learning. We can stand up and pledge allegiance every day, "with liberty and justice for all," but it's a big lie if "all" don't include blacks and everybody else.

And what's to be done? It's the disenfranchisement that Odell explained about. All the niceness in the world isn't going to change the fact that whites have privileges. If we had a crystal ball showing us the date when everything would be all equaled up, would that make it better? Or a measuring stick that showed how far we've come and how far we've yet to go? But how far *have* we come, when black people are still being lynched and Foster's afraid to go to a baseball game?

We roll along past the parking lot to the red-brick stadium. I tell Foster all about how me and Da kiss the paver stone by the edge of the southeast wall. Da says Mr. Comiskey buried a brick painted green with a shamrock right there. A brick all the way from Ireland. Just for luck.

My da told me the commissioner made the White Sox play their first game of the season on a Friday, which canceled all the luck, seeing as how Fridays are bad luck. But with us kissing the stone, the luck is restored. 'Course today is also a Friday, so I say a quick Hail Mary that bringing Da to the game will be extra lucky.

"Come on," I say to Foster, pointing at the paver stone.

"Nah," he says. "I ain't superstitious."

Now that's a downright lie and I know it, as he's always pitching pennies in the river for luck, but I keep my mouth shut. I just kiss the paver three times, for me and Da and Foster.

I frown at him. "If the Sox don't win, it'll be your fault."

I notice the lines of fans at the stadium. Ladies in dresses, holding on to the arms of their fellows. Men in suits, smoking cigars. Families with kids in short pants. It's a sea of hats. And under every hat is a white face.

Puffy red faces. Pimply white faces. Creamy peach faces. Even some toasty tan with beaky noses, but no dark brown. Is Foster right? Can they stop black people from going to baseball games? Is it like Odell says—the hate like the rocks, under the surface of the river, that nobody sees but everybody knows about?

I take over pushing Da and steer around to the gate nearest the outfield. The ice is all gone and Da looks mighty hot again.

I stop in a little spot of shade and pull Foster over.

"Okay," I tell him. "So you're right. Like you said,

mostly white folks are going to the game. What do you want to do?"

"I'll go home." Foster shades his eyes, watching all the excited fans streaming into the park.

"Don't you want to see the game?"

"Sure, but . . ." His eyes get wishful for a second, but then he shakes his head.

"Then why you want to leave?"

"Some things ain't worth it, Billy." He folds his arms across his chest. "They just ain't worth it."

"Well, this is. This is one of them doors of opportunity, like Mr. Doo Boo says."

Foster's gloomy expression changes to a grin. "It's Du Bois, a French name. Wait until I tell my daddy you called him Doo Boo!"

"Well, whatever his name is, are you coming or not?"

Foster grabs hold of the wheelchair and we follow the crowd. People give us cuts when they see Da in his wheelchair, and before we know it, we're almost to the gate.

I see people nod in my direction and I start to get mighty puffed up. *Yes*, I think. *That's me. Billy the do-gooder, taking my war hero da and my black friend to a game.* But then I notice people are leaving a wide space behind us. Is that on account of the wheelchair? Or Foster? Maybe they're shaking their heads, disappointed with me. Maybe I'm Billy the selfish boy, putting his da and his friend in danger.

I take a deep breath and decide I don't much care. We're White Sox fans, come to watch the White Sox game, and that's that.

I dig in my pocket and fish out seventy-five cents for three bleacher seats. The man at the gate rips the corners off the tickets and gives me the stubs, and I hand Foster one of them. He pulls out a little leather pouch and slides the ticket stub inside.

"What's that?" I ask.

"Lucky stuff."

"I thought you weren't superstitious."

"I ain't. I just collect lucky stuff."

I shake my head and start to argue, but we're inside the park and the noise takes over. We're pushed along, like logs on the river, into the gray concrete cavern, cooler and darker than the hot sidewalks.

Foster pulls his cap down low over his eyes and tucks his hands up into his sleeves and for a minute I'm sorry I ever thought of the idea. It takes both of us to push Da up the ramp. When we get to the first level, we walk out into the sunshine again.

The concession area is full to brimming with people.

And who do I see but my old friends from Nativity, Kevin and Connor, standing with Timmy in the hot dog line. I think how we all used to go to the games with our das, when we were little shavers. It makes me miss the old times.

"Want a hot dog?" I ask Foster.

"Now?"

"Before we get Da to the bleachers. It'll be easier."

I help Foster park Da in a little corner, away from the crowd and out of my old friends' sight.

"Stay here," I tell him.

"Why?"

"Keep Da in the shade. I'll be right back," I say, and I go get in line.

Kevin sees me first. "Hey Billy, who you with? Thought you had to take care of your da?"

"Nobody. Ma give me the day off." It's just a little lie. I tell myself I'm doing it to protect Foster. But maybe that's another lie.

Timmy says, "You shoulda gone to the Cubs game three weeks ago."

"I don't go for the Cubs," I tell him. What's wrong with him? He knows that. It's only been four days since he called me a yellow-bellied sissy and he's acting like he don't know me?

He waits until Kevin and Connor are looking at him, then he says, "No? Well that's when Ladies' Day was. Sorry you missed it."

The three of them split their guts laughing. I get it. Timmy's still blaming me for being a sissy, but I give him a skunk eye and don't crack a smile. Connor socks my arm. "We're sitting over there, if you want to come by." He points beyond first base.

"I will," I say. "Thanks." Another lie. I pay the vendor ten cents for each hot dog and five cents for each root beer. I have a nickel left. Cracker Jacks, I decide. No, maybe popcorn. Or a scorecard.

"Make up your mind, sonny." The vendor drums his fingers on the edge of the booth.

Da always gets a scorecard. "To prove to your Ma we was at the game and not the pub." And he laughs at his own joke.

But I ain't sure how to fill out the scorecard by myself, so I get the Cracker Jacks. Everything goes into a box, and I make Foster carry it while I push Da.

When we get to the bleachers we go down another ramp to the wooden benches. Right away I notice some other black folks already in the bleachers, maybe ten. I poke Foster with my elbow and nod toward them.

"See?"

He nods toward the entire ballpark, filling up with gazillions of people, all the same color as me. "See?" he says.

I teach Da how to eat his hot dog, but he bites off way too much and can't chew. Then the straw comes out of the cup and he waves it around in his teeth, not sure how to put it back in the cup. I sigh. Maybe Foster's right. Maybe some things aren't worth it.

I stand Da up to sing "The Star-Spangled Banner" and I see tears in his eyes. Then the White Sox take the field. Lefty Williams strides up to the mound and lets one fly. *Stee-rike!* On second thought, maybe some things *are* worth it.

All around us people are using their scorecards to fan themselves. It's hotter than hot. Lefty struggles to keep the ball in the strike zone and wipes his forehead. Schalk walks out to the mound. Bronkie has a full count, then pounds one to right field. Gedeon walks. Bronkie tries to steal and gets picked off. After three balls to Jacobson, Lefty looks flustered. Then Jacobson grounds one to second. Double play.

The White Sox are up but do nothing. First inning, no score.

Fans are riled. Sisler is up. Before we know what's

happened he's got a full count. Lefty pitches. It's low but Sisler swings for the back fence. Holy cow. It's gone—no, wait—back, back, back—Joe's running hard. He's got it! Whoopee!

Lefty steps off the mound and stretches his arm. Kenny Williams from the Browns strides to the plate. We're all sweating. Lefty wipes his brow, then pulls something from under his hat and palms the ball.

"That's a spitball," I whisper to Foster. "Look, it's Lefty Williams versus Kenny Williams, all your kin."

"You're funny," he says. "Funny lookin'."

Williams is at the plate. He churns the bat, waiting. Lefty launches the ball. Williams connects. *Crack!* The ball sails up and up and up. It's a home run for sure. The crowd groans and we watch Williams—Kenny Williams, that is—saunter around the bases.

Lefty is not on the money today. Maybe it's the heat. Maybe it's Friday's bad luck. He pitches to Smith, who gets a single. Gerber goes the full count and it looks grim, but he gets caught on a changeup.

Two outs. Severeid hauls off and swings at the first pitch. I look down for a second and when I look back up, Lefty is lying on the ground and the fans are screaming.

"What happened?" I yell at Foster.

"Hit. Got his hand up there just in time." Foster points to his temple.

I shudder. Gosh. Lefty is the best.

Severeid is at second base before the manager can get to the mound. Lefty is still. No one in the stands makes a sound or moves a muscle. It's creepy. There's a crowd of managers and players around Lefty, but we can see his legs splayed out to the side. We hold our hands above our eyebrows, straining to see. The flags on top of the stadium roof hang limp. Not a breeze stirs the air. We're all in a moving picture that stopped in the middle of the reel.

"He moved his leg," the man behind me says. "Look, he moved."

We stand on our tiptoes to try to get a look. Then, sure enough, Lefty is sitting up, slowly at first. The managers help pull him to his feet. The stands break out in cheers as he wobble-walks to the bench.

We sigh and sit back down. What a relief! But jeez Louise, now it seems even hotter. Da's red in the face and breathing hard. I take off his hat and see his hair all plastered to his head with sweat. We finish off our root beers before the second inning ends, and I'm out of money. I take our cups and leave to get water while Foster keeps an eye on Da.

'Course, while I'm hunting for the sinks to get the water, the White Sox score and I miss it. Now it's two to one. I finally find the privies and fill our cups. My cheeks feel prickly and I look in the mirror. Fresh new dots of freckles sprinkle across my nose toward my pink, sunburned cheeks. Well, there's nothing to do about it now but pull my cap down as far as it can go. I wonder about Foster and sunburn. I balance the cups and rush back.

And so it goes. Five innings are over and the score is four to three. So far no home runs for the White Sox, but Happy's scored and so has Shoeless Joe. Joe backs up for a ball and I yell, "Come on, Joe, give it the green!"

When Schalk gets up to bat, my da yells out, "Give it the green, Cracker!" Me and Foster about fall out of our seats laughing. I explain that they call Ray Schalk "Cracker" 'cause he's built like a cracker box. It's the first words my da's ever said since he's been home. He'll be back to normal soon, I just know it.

I feel pretty good about my plan. So far it's landing more on the great side than on the terrible side. Ma will see how swell everything went and she won't be mad. She could even come next time. The whole family. And Foster and his brothers. His daddy too.

Foster interrupts my thinking. "I gotta go."

"We just got here," I say, turning to look at him.

"No. I gotta go. You know. *Go.*"

"Well, go. The privy is up there." I point.

"I ain't going by myself."

"You don't need me to go with you—they're right there."

Foster stares at me hard, like I have a rock for a brain. Then he gets up, saying, "Excuse me" to the other people on the bench. It isn't until he stalks off I figure it out. He wasn't afraid of getting lost. He was afraid of all the white people. That's why he wanted me to go with him.

Well, it's too late now, and anyway it's not worth dragging Da back into the wheelchair just for a trip to the privy. I tell myself not to worry.

The whole sixth inning goes by, and the top of the seventh, and by the seventh-inning stretch I realize he's still gone. I still ain't real worried. I figure he snuck down to the lower levels to try and get a close look at the White Sox bench, like I always do. I hope he can see who's warming up to pitch next.

There's a meeting on the mound and the Browns' pitcher is helped off the field. The announcer says he's suffering from heatstroke. The score is still four to three. Maybe the White Sox will score in the bottom of the seventh. The lucky seventh inning.

I loosen Da's tie and fan him some more. If I didn't know better I'd think Da had just finished ten rounds with Jack Dempsey, his face is so puffy and red.

Still no Foster. He's been gone a long time. More than a half hour. I decide I better go find him. I may as well be an old nanny, looking after my old Da and my dimwit friend, Foster.

I help Da back into the wheelchair and a couple of nice blokes lift it up to the walkway for me. Da seems to have gained twenty pounds of dead weight. Pushing him takes all I got. When we finally get to the privies I find that the wheelchair won't fit through the door. Jeez Louise. I leave Da and open the door, hollering for Foster.

No answer.

Now what?

There's more facilities on the other side and I check them all. No Foster. I find an usher watching the entrance to the lower box seats.

"Excuse me. My friend went to the privy, and now I can't find him. I checked all the ones on this level."

"Did you check the one down there?" He points down a hallway that's hidden from the main ramp.

"Thanks," I say, and I wheel Da down there as fast as

I can, leave him in the hallway, and push open the privy door. "Foster! Foster!"

"Billy. Help me. Billy." A soft voice bleats out my name.

One of the stall doors is closed tight, but no feet are showing underneath. I shimmy under and look up—and there's Foster. His white shirt has spots of blood on it, and his lip is swollen up like a bee stung him. I can't believe it.

He's hanging by his collar from the hook on the back of the door. His knees are bent with his feet pressed flat against the door to hold himself up. But even as I watch he loses his grip and his body drops down, the shirt cutting into his neck, pinching the circulation from his arms.

I grab his legs and squat down. "Here. Stand on my shoulders," I tell him.

He balances on my shoulders and unbuttons his shirt, then slowly climbs off and sinks to the floor. His leather pouch is lying on the ground and I pick it up. His lucky stuff is dumped out all around it. I stick it all back in, looking at it as I do.

His White Sox ticket stub.

A picture of his family.

There's even some of the things I put in our secret hiding spot:

A black marble, with a white-center eye.

A button from an American Legion uniform, a star surrounded by rings of blue and gold.

A homecoming football badge from the University of Illinois.

Then I see a folded-up note. I keep my back to him and open it, sneaky-like. It's a map of Bubbly Creek and the lean-to that I drew in class one day. Sometime since, he's added the raft and written PRIDE OF THE RIVER in a bubble hovering above it. I look closer. Written straight as an arrow are the letters WJM and FJW, our initials, one on the front of the raft and one on the back. And across the middle he's added BEST FRIENDS.

My back prickles. He doesn't deserve a lousy friend like me.

I quickly refold the map, put it in the pouch, and give it all back to Foster.

"They stole my Confederate dollar, and my Buffalo nickel," he says. "And my pocketknife."

"Who?"

"They told me to tell you they was friends of Mickey."

My stomach gets hard and my jaw gets tight. This has to be Timmy's fault. I'm going to the usher. They'll see. They can't mess with me and my friend. There's laws, ain't there? Laws for protecting people. I grab Foster by the arm and pull him up, and together we bust out the bathroom door.

Immediately, I forget all about the usher. Da's head is tilted down almost to his knees. There's a wet spot spreading across his lap and down the inside of his pants leg. At first I think he's barfed up his lunch, and then with a shooting pinch of regret I realize that in all the trips to privies I forgot to take him.

I rush over and pat his back. "Da. Da. You're okay. You're okay." My poor da. I know my great thing is over now and it feels more terrible than great. We walk home, Foster's swollen lip and Da's wet lap making my heart flip-flop.

Just as we head out of the park and down Thirty-Fifth, a huge roar erupts from the Baseball Palace of the World. It can only mean one thing, but we'll have to wait to find out in the papers.

Chapter Twelve

I WAKE UP THINKING ABOUT Lefty Williams, hoping he's not bad hurt. I was considering joining the White Sox, maybe even pitching for them. But that seems too dangerous, now. Jeez Louise. Maybe I'll do something safer. Work for the railroad or be a banker or something.

Not even a breath of air is coming through our bedroom window.

On second thought, even a banker's job can be risky on account of that accident last Monday. Nine bankers killed by the Goodyear Blimp that floated on that puff of breeze right into the Illinois Trust and Savings Bank.

The *Wingfoot Express*. Every day the papers talk about it. Lots of people stood right there on the street and saw it go down. Burning up. Everybody on it died except for the pilot, who landed with his parachute on the roof of the Board of Trade Building. The switchboard operator at the bank said, "There was a shadow and I looked up to the roof."

And that roof was made of glass panes all put together to make a giant skylight. The burning blimp came crashing through that skylight. The fuel tanks exploded when they hit the floor, making it so hot all the glass melted and showered down. Some guy yelled out, "My God, it's raining hell."

I read that part of the story a couple of times. How many people can say that in their lifetime? "My God, it's raining hell." And six hours later, they made a new law about flying over the city. Seems new laws always come after bad things happen.

Life sure is unpredictable, or risky, as I always say. Full of those land mines.

Like those "friends of Mickey's" beating up Foster at the ball game. I got to keep a better eye out, I think to myself. Protect my family and friends. Like I promised Ma. And I aim to. Just let me hear Mickey say one more thing like "trouble is coming," and this time I aim to tell

Officer O'Brien. If he don't listen, well then, he's not the only copper, is he? And the same for that conniving Mr. Weinstein. It's time I got to the truth before it's too late.

"Billy, get up. Ma wants to talk to you."

Well, don't that figure. Speaking of laws getting made after bad things happen.

Mr. Weinstein nods at me when I walk into the kitchen and Da sings out, "Give it the green!" The heavenly smell of fresh scones takes a little of the edge off my worries.

Ma pours tea into their cups and shakes her head. "He's been at it since he woke up. First words he says and they're about baseball? Humph. I don't know how you can play baseball and watch Da and Anna at the same time." She whisks the scones off the baking sheet without a hot pad, cooling her hot fingers by flicking the air. "Don't take him and Anna out today," she says. "It's too hot."

"Aw, Ma." I breathe a secret sigh of relief that all she thinks is that I took Da and Anna to watch *me* play baseball. She doesn't know. Nobody knows. Only Da and Foster.

Mary is giving me the evil eye. Maybe Mary knows. *Aw, go soak your head, Mary*, I think. But Mary makes me think of Mickey and his threat, and that makes me worried for Foster and his family.

"Billy, are you listening to me?"

"Yes, Ma."

"I'm working breakfast and lunch at the diner. What with the strikers and the heat, we've been busy morning and noon. We're going to Mass tonight, so tomorrow me and the ladies can start getting things in order for the parish fair. Saints alive, it's next week, already."

Ma heaves a big sigh and kisses the top of Da's head. Her damp hair makes little curls stick to her red face.

"I'm sorry, Billy," she says, turning back to me and softening. "Taking away from your Saturday. You can play tomorrow, even though it's Sunday, and Mary can watch the both of them."

Mary narrows her eyelids and squints at me. "Oh, no, I can't," she says.

"Don't you get all high and mighty, Miss Mary. All week you make money at the Dolans' doing very little but sitting on your sweet behind, bless their generosity, so you can use a wee smidgen of your time to help out your own family."

Mary stomps off to the bedroom and Ma keeps right on talking to me.

"Timmy's ma was asking if you wanted to go to the beach with Timmy and his da tomorrow. She said Timmy felt poorly yesterday, but he might be better by tomorrow."

"Sure, Ma. Sure."

"And mind you, don't you get into trouble."

"I won't." I turn around so nobody can see the grin on my face. I'm about to bust. *Freedom!* No Anna. No Da. For a whole day. Nobody to worry about. And on a Sunday, too. Family day. Well, Katy bar the door! The church ladies are getting ready for the fair!

But I ain't going anywhere with Timmy and his da. No sir. It's time to test that raft. Give it a trial. In case Mickey and his friends ever try anything else like what they done to Foster yesterday. Me and my best friend, we'll be like all those people in Georgia who just up and disappeared in the night to save themselves from being lynched.

Besides, it's time to give those boring landlubbers some fun for their money. I aim to do it. I know on Sundays Foster's daddy goes to church, but he don't make his boys go along, seeing as how afterwards he goes to see their auntie. If there's a better way to spend a Sunday, I don't know it.

Mr. Weinstein interrupts my thoughts and hands me the newspaper. "Look. You Vite Zoak."

I have no idea what he's talking about, but then I see the headline:

EVERYTHING GOES WRONG BUT SOX WIN THE SAME.

6–4. "They won, Da. They won!" I plop right down and devour the article. Well, sure enough. SOX SEW IT UP IN THE EIGHTH, I read. That's what we heard while we was walking away with Foster's fat lip and Da's wet pants.

Just my luck. Next time I ain't leaving until they pull up the bases.

A little hiccup in my stomach reminds me that it was partly my fault we had to leave the game. Serves me right for making Foster go alone to the privy and completely forgetting my da needed to use it at all. If only I thought about others for a change. If only. Father Flaherty says the If-Only bricks and the Good-Intention bricks pave the road to hell, and the Good-Deed bricks pave the road to heaven.

I say a promise to myself that next time I will think more about others than the three in one. Me, myself, and I.

I don't think Timmy's old joke is so funny anymore. Never did, really. 'Course I used to laugh a little, but I worried God heard our disrespect—our blasphemy, as Ma would call it.

A sour-milk feeling creeps into my stomach. I wonder if Timmy is the "friend of Mickey's" that strung Foster up. My double-crossing, disrespecting, no-count old friend Timmy, who wants me to go to the beach on Sunday with him and his da. His da, who can't shut up about the strikers and the scabs.

I been doing a lot of puzzling about it. Here's what I think. Let's say one day the baseball players want better dugouts and more money, so they go to the owners and the owners say no. Then the baseball players say they ain't going to play unless the owners change their mind. So the owners go on out and find some fellows who been wanting to play baseball but ain't had a chance on account of the regular players taking the jobs. The owners hire those new players to play 'cause they're just happy to play, and the owners don't got to pay them more money or fancy up the dugouts to get 'em to. Then the regular players get all riled up and start fighting the new players for taking their spots on the team. But whose fault is it, really?

It's the owners they should be fighting, not the new players. I wish I had the guts to tell Mr. Beatty what I think.

All day me and Anna and Da stay in the house, watching the thunderclouds march across the sky, pelting everybody's Saturday with rain while Ma and Mr. Weinstein spend half their weekend working. I decide this is my opportunity to do some spying on the spy living in my house. I feel a little guilty after he was so excited to share the news about the White Sox with me. But that's what spies do, ain't it? They make you trust them, and then they betray you. I got to keep my family safe, no matter what, like I promised myself I would. Last time Ma changed the linens in Mr. Weinstein's room I saw where she put the key.

I get Anna to play hide-and-go-seek, and when it's my turn to hide, I pull the key from the drawer in the buffet and sneak into Mr. Weinstein's room. It's off limits and I know it, but won't Ma be happy when I'm the hero for saving the neighborhood?

The blanket on his bed is smooth as ice, with the corners tucked under just so. He has a blue-and-silver picture frame on the nightstand, and an alarm clock. I pick up the frame. Each corner has a pattern of silver vines that trail out from silver roses. Two boys in black suits stand behind a lady with a black scarf and a man with a broom-bristle beard. *Mr. Weinstein's family,* I think. I peer closer and guess that the younger boy might be Mr. Weinstein, because his hair isn't as curly as the other boy's. I turn the frame over and flip the little hinged stand to the side. The photograph comes loose and on the back this is what I see: Семейство Вайнштейнхе 1901. I ain't ever seen communist writing, but I'm almost positive that's what it looks like. I quick put the photo back in and carefully stand the frame back up.

I open the drawer in the dresser—what used to be my junk drawer. Just three things are placed there, side by side:

A brown leather book with gold, faded trim.

A wooden cigar box.

A chipped ceramic bowl with coins in it.

I thumb through the pages of the book. All strange writing, like on the back of the picture.

I open the cigar box. A sweet, grassy, moldy smell makes my nose wrinkle. On the inside cover is a grand baseball park picture—keen, as Foster says. I look again at the box. NATIONAL LEAGUE, HOMERS, it reads. I sure would like to ask Mr. Weinstein for this box when he's done smoking his cigars. I look back in the box and decide to put a cigar into my pocket. He won't miss one. And he can't smoke in the house, anyway. Wait until I show Foster and Odell. We can pass it around at Bubbly Creek.

The coins are copper and silver. The copper coins are the size of quarters and have plant designs on them. The silver coins are like my silver dollars, but with a bearded man on them and strange writing all around the edges. I slip one of the silver coins into my pocket. I ain't a thief. It's just for investigation purposes. And I bet Foster has never seen Russian spy money. Won't he get a surprise when he finds this in our secret hiding spot?

Then I remember that Anna counts awful quick and not too high, so I lickety-split hide in the closet, careful not to disturb Mr. Weinstein's shiny black shoes, the toes lined up like soldiers.

So far I haven't found any spy gear. No disguises. No fake passports. No acid. No dynamite.

I take a deep breath and tilt my head back, holding in the sweet cigar smell and the fresh shoe polish. The shelf above my head is empty, except for a shoe box. A shoe box? A shoe box! Maybe the same shoe box he took out of that car. Maybe he keeps his spy stuff in there. Maybe his bomb-making supplies. I can't reach the shoe box, and before I can figure out how to get it down, I hear Anna.

"Ready or not, here I come. Where are you, Billy?"

I hear Anna walk down the hall. First she opens the door to the bedroom we share. "Bill-eeee. Bill-eeee." She sings my name.

She's back in the hall. Then she opens Mr. Weinstein's door.

Everything is so quiet my breathing sounds like a dragon's. This is how I will be when I'm a soldier. The enemy will walk so close to me and right when they get two inches away I will—

Anna opens the closet door and I jump out. "Arghhhhh!"

I yell. She screams and runs away, wailing, and I double over, laughing hysterically.

And that's when I see there's a suitcase under Mr. Weinstein's bed. I'm in luck. I can use it to reach the shoe box. In my head I can already hear Police Chief Garrity congratulating me when I turn Mr. Weinstein in: *Thank you, Billy. He's a tough nut and you cracked him. Cracked the case wide open. For the loveamike, I don't know how you did it, but there's job waiting for you with the Chicago police when you're older.*

I pull the suitcase over to the closet and position it under the shoe box. My heart is hammering and a bead of sweat trickles down my spine as I put first one foot, and then the other on top of the brown leather, then pull the shoe box down.

It's tied shut with a string, and the knot is tight, so I put the box on the bed and sneak across the hall to get my pocketknife. Then I sneak back into Mr. Weinstein's room, lifting up on the knob so it doesn't even make a click when the door shuts. One of my own spy techniques.

I poke and wiggle my knife into the knot and loosen it, without cutting the string. Then I slide the string off the box.

What do spies keep in shoe boxes? Money? Stolen passports? Russian spy books?

I open the lid.

It takes me a second to recognize what I see. A revolver. An honest-to-goodness revolver. It's almost as long as the shoe box. Black and dangerous-looking.

I put my finger on the metal. It's cold.

I lift the end of the handle. It's heavy.

Aha! I think. *The weapon of a spy.*

A chill slides down my spine. How many poor souls did Mr. Weinstein send to the ever-after if they refused to betray their country? What if he finds out I know about his secret activities? I take the gun from the box and a little tin with bullets spills open.

I hold the gun steady. I'm the cowboy outlaw, Billy the Kid. I'm the mobster boss, Johnny Torrio. I'm John J. Garrity, Chicago police chief, protecting my city. I'm aiming bravely at my imaginary enemy when the door opens— *BLAM!*—and Anna is pointing at me, with Da next to her in his wheelchair.

I jerk back in surprise. My finger pulls the trigger and the loudest sound I ever heard explodes in the room.

Whole circuses of things happen at once.

I fling the gun from my hand and drop to the floor.

Anna screams.

My da shouts out, "Billy!"

And I smell firecrackers.

It feels like a year before I open my eyes and wiggle my fingers and my nose. I'm not dead.

Not yet, anyway. Not until Ma finds out what I done.

The gun is lying three feet away from my head. I shiver when I look at it, a metal monster that could of killed me.

Anna is still screaming, her mouth shaped in a perfect circle, and her eyes squeezed shut tight. Da's shoulders are shaking up and down. I get up, kind of wobbly, and walk over to him. He's crying. Tears just streaming down his cheeks.

"I'm sorry, Da. I'm sorry." I throw my arms around his neck.

"Billy. Billy." He says it like he's never said it before. Like it's a new flavor rolling around on his tongue.

Anna's saucer eyes stare at me and her lip is quivering. I stoop down and hug her. "It's okay, Anna. Nothing happened."

"Billy." My da pulls on my sleeve and points at the gun. He motions for me to get it.

I shudder and go back into Mr. Weinstein's room to pick it up, holding it far away from me, pointed down. My da takes it and after a few tries manages to pop open the part that spins. He dumps the bullets out into his lap and with a shaky hand gives me the gun. I gather up the bullets with my own shaking hands.

When I put the gun back in the box I see the hole in the white blanket, black powder all around it, and I know I'm a goner.

I push my da's wheelchair back to the front room. After a few minutes my da says, "Billy."

I look up and see he's holding his arm up with his hand pointed like a gun. And he laughs. For the first time in forever.

And I laugh, too, my heart still pounding—from fear, but also from hope, because the laughing makes me think my old da might be really be coming back to me.

And besides, I might as well laugh now. Once Ma finds out what happened, my laughing days will be over.

"Jaysus, Mary, and the wee donkey, what is the matter with you?" Ma says when she hears about it. "Mr. Weinstein—a Russian spy? He *escaped* from Russia, Billy. They would have killed him. And you—making him afraid in his very own home!"

"But I seen him making a bomb. Wires and white powder and such."

"Sure. And he put that bomb right back into my carpet

sweeper did he? After he took it apart and cleaned the brush, using up his fancy wires from his railroad job, digging out the dirt you drag in from God knows where? As a favor to me he did it, seeing as it couldn't pick up the sugar from the sugar bowl I tipped over that day." She shakes her head. "Ah Billy, for the life of me."

She makes me wash all Mr. Weinstein's sheets and remake the bed. The bullet went clear through to the floor. I get the willies when I think it came close to going clear through me.

Ma and Mr. Weinstein exchange some pretty loud words when he gets home from work. Then she comes and demands that I put the cigar and the coin back. "You thieving scalawag, you," she cries. "Have you no shame? If Mr. Weinstein moves out on account of your nonsense, you won't be eating for a week."

After she's done with me, I walk slowly down the hall and knock on Mr. Weinstein's door.

"Come," he says, in such a low voice I can barely hear him.

He's sitting on the edge of his bed, his head in his hands. He doesn't look at me.

I hold out the cigar and the coin. "I didn't mean anything by it. Honest. Swear on the Bible."

Mr. Weinstein lifts his head and I see so much sadness in his eyes that my heart squeezes. He holds out his hand. His long fingers shake as I lay the cigar and the coin in his palm.

"You think you know me. A spy, you think." He closes his fist around the cigar and the coin and raises it to the level of my eyes. "You know nothing of me. Nothing of what I lost. My wife. My family. All I own." He drops his fist and opens his hand. The cigar rolls onto his lap. "I lost everything. Then I come here. To make a new life. To be free. To have rights."

"I'm sorry," I whisper, the tips of my ears burning. When he's silent for another minute, I tiptoe out. I'm so ashamed. What was I thinking, hurting a man just for being different? Going on assumptions instead of finding out the facts.

Mary is changing in the bedroom and I can hear Ma whispering to Da in the front room. The ringing in my ears from the gunshot won't stop. I sigh and slip down to sit cross-legged on the floor in the hall, not welcome anywhere. I'm no better than Mickey and them Hamburgs. No better than Timmy's da. And I sure ain't no hero.

While we're at Mass that night, I think about running away. Could go down South to visit Foster's family. Could go north to Canada where maybe color don't matter so much.

Or maybe to Ireland and meet my relatives. Somewhere far away, where nobody knows what a louse I am.

But I'm pretty sure I won't be joining up for the next war. Especially not in the Field Artillery. One near miss with death is plenty enough for me. I shudder, thinking about the explosion the gun made when it went off. Maybe Ma is right. Maybe there won't be another war. One Great War might be enough.

Making a big mistake has lots of little aftershocks. I disappointed Ma. I scared Anna. I hurt Mr. Weinstein. I told a lie to my friends, and Ma says that's the same as blowing on a dandelion weed. One puff and the seeds can't ever be collected again.

Floating away on a raft seems mighty tempting right now. Maybe I should just let her loose, climb aboard, and disappear before Foster and Odell and Emmett find out what I done, how wrong I was.

When I'm lying in bed after Mass I hear Mary sneak back into the bedroom. It's after midnight and I can't sleep.

"Mary," I whisper.

"What?"

"I didn't mean to shoot the gun." My voice cracks a bit and I clear my throat, so it don't sound like I'm crying.

"Why'd you go in his room?"

"Looking for evidence. I thought he was a spy."

"He's not a spy, Billy," says Mary. "Ma says he's a Jew. A Russian Jew."

A Jew? Suddenly the last clues click into place. The black book with foreign writing. The strange coins. Not eating our ham. The Easter egg reminding him of the seder meal. Of course. It makes sense now.

But why didn't Mary tell me? It was me and Mary first decided Mr. Weinstein was a Russian spy, making up code words and peeking at him through cracks in doors. We kept all the facts about him in Mary's diary, all written in our secret language.

I guess everyone just up and turned into grown-ups while I stayed a baby, building forts and sneaking into the bedrooms of Russian Jews.

I turn over and ball the pillow up under my head. "Mary?"

"Go to sleep, Billy."

"Do girls like boys who go to war?"

Mary doesn't answer for a long minute. Then, in a soft voice, she says, "They don't have to go to war. They just have to be brave."

"Like Joey, your fellow you meet under the stairs?"

"Are you spying on me now, too? I thought you promised." Mary turns her back to me.

"You mean Dynamite Joey. That's what Mickey calls him." My whispering gets louder. "So it's brave to blow up a bunch of garter snakes with a firecracker? And throw a bottle at a little kid and his puppy? 'Cause that's what he done. I seen him."

Mary flips around and rises up on her elbow. "Oh, what do you know? His name is Joseph. Joseph Brooks. And he's brave, all right. He might join Ragen's Colts and dump Mickey and his Hamburgs. Joseph's tougher than Mickey, that's for sure."

"How's that?"

"He says any man even looks at me, he'll shoot him dead."

"Why can't people look at you?" I ask.

"They can. 'Cause I'm pretty. Joseph says. But he's my fellow now, so they can't. He punched a black man just for walking too close to me."

"Why'd he do that?"

"Protecting me, mostly. Plus, Joey's a union man, and the union says blacks are garbage scabs."

Timmy and his da talk the same way. Blacks willing to work when the union members are striking for better pay. Just like that rich Mr. Swift hired those blacks as long as they didn't join the union. I guess that would make me

mad, too. And who's the big winner? The company owners, that's who. All sunny-side-up that the work is getting
done and they don't have to fork out any more money to
the strikers.

I lean up on one elbow just like Mary, and search for her
face in the dark. "But if the unions let the blacks join, then
they won't be scabs." Foster is the one who explained this to
me. And then I read it in *The Chicago Defender*. The one I
keep hidden between the mattress and the bed slats.

"What are you, Billy? One of them you-know-what
lovers? Don't you get it? Those blacks are Bolsheviks and
communists, all of them. They're destroying our country.
President Wilson even said so."

I'm more worried than ever about Foster and his family. If all of Chicago is out to get them, they won't stand a
chance. *The Chicago Defender* says Big Bill is all blow and
no go. And if President Wilson can't even take care of his
own backyard in Washington, DC, then it's up to me to
keep an eye out. And my ears open. I might have to do
more than warn them. I might have to protect them. And
that's a promise. Them politicians might not keep their
promises, but I aim to keep mine.

Chapter Thirteen

SUNDAY COMES, AND IT'S HOTTER than every day before it. It seems a shame to waste so much heat in the summer when all winter we shiver and blow on our fingers to keep warm. But still there's no greater feeling than knowing a day is stretched out in front of you, just waiting for you to walk into it. I got no Da and no Anna to watch today, so I'm free as free can be.

I get up before Mary and Anna to help Ma put together some breakfast. I start the kettle and set out the cups, slice the leftover scones, and plop some grease in the frying pan. When Ma comes into the kitchen she cups my chin in her hand.

"You're a special son, now, you are, Billy. But you made a terrible mistake yesterday."

My heart drops fifty feet. *She's going to punish me by making me stay in the house all day. She's taking my one free day away.*

"What you did was wrong, but your da smiling and starting to speak sure makes me think there was some right come out of it." She lets me go and sets the scones into the grease. "What do you think?" And before I can answer she pulls me in for a hug. "Sometimes I think you're off with the fairies, that's what I think. You've quit the spy business, have you?"

I nod my head and hold my breath for luck.

"And you can stay out of trouble for one whole day, can you?"

I nod again and cross my fingers.

"All right, then. Be sure to thank your da and Mr. Weinstein for putting in a good word for you." She winks at me and while she flips the scones over, I hand her the eggs, the silliest grin on my face.

Da wheels into the kitchen with his nose twitching and a smile on his face, and Mr. Weinstein comes next. I know how they feel. Scones with butter and jam are fine, but a scone fried up to dip in ketchup, with a nice buttery egg on the side—well that just makes the world go round.

Ma pours the tea, and after I wolf down my breakfast, she asks me to run her baskets down to the church for the parish fair. "Be sure to thank Timmy's da for taking you to the beach. And keep your shirt on in the water so you don't get burned." She tries to give me a kiss, but Da and Mr. Weinstein are watching so I duck under her and grab her baskets, bounding out the door and down the steps.

The parish fair comes around once a year, and all the ladies make stuff to sell. Stuff like pot holders and aprons, and of course food. Ma's whipped up a basket full of fresh scones and homemade jam, plus cans of stuff for the oyster stew.

I wonder who's running for the oysters, since Da can't do it anymore. Prolly Mr. Beatty, if he's sober, or Officer O'Brien.

Ma's already gone to the church when I get back, even though I took the alley shortcuts. It's too early to head to Foster's, but I don't want to get stuck in the house, so I fish around in my drawer for my baseball cards and take them out to the front stoop. I have three kinds of cards: my da's White Borders, my own Zeenuts from the Cracker Jacks boxes, and the set I got for Christmas from the Boston Store.

From the stoop I can see the steeples of three churches

and hear the whistle of the train that brings all the ball players to Chicago, with its steak dinners and special cars for gambling. Riding the rails in style, they say.

I think about Foster and his family traveling all the way to Chicago with just what they could carry. Not knowing where to find their kin. All of them working or going to school, just to live in a shanty by the river.

Life is chancy, I guess. Risky, even. And a lot depends on which side of the line you're born on. Seems like there's more land mines on one side than the other.

I sort my cards into three piles: best, okay, and lousy. I have three players I consider best. Only three: Babe Ruth, Joe Jackson, and Smoky Joe Wood. Smoky Joe used to be the best pitcher in the league, until he hurt his thumb. Now he's an outfielder, and a really good hitter.

I have Ty Cobb, the Georgia Peach, who's a good ball player, but on account of his personality I put him in the okay pile. He's got a really bad temper, even attacked a crippled man in the stands once. And some say he's a racist, too. I know he joined up and went to war, though, so I guess he's got some good qualities mixed in with the bad.

My lousy pile is stacked three inches high when I'm done. And in all my cards I only have five White Sox players. That's prolly why the piles are so lopsided. Last two times I plunked down my nickels for Cracker Jacks, I got no White Sox player cards at all. There should be a rule. If you buy Cracker Jacks in your hometown they oughta put your hometown baseball players' cards in the box.

If only I had the money for a new set. They used to put cards in the cigarette packs, but Da don't smoke anymore.

If only Da could stay home alone so I could make some deliveries for Mr. O'Doulle or go off to the docks and work for tips.

If only. There it is again. And if only the White Sox make it to the World Series. That would really be something.

Mary comes out on the stoop with a book. "What're you doing?" she asks.

"Sorting baseball cards. Want to borrow some to play with Da?"

She doesn't answer, just stares off at the city, her eyes getting kind of glassy. "Billy, do you ever wish you were born a girl?"

"Are you off with the fairies?" I cry. "Why ever would I want to be a girl? They get stuck in the house, don't play baseball, and wear skirts."

Mary sighs. She looks at her feet. After a minute, she says, "I wish I was born a boy."

"So you could play baseball?"

"No, so I could protect myself."

"But you got Joey," I say.

She continues with a pitiful voice, "And so I'd for sure get to go to a good high school. And maybe college."

"You can do that now," I say.

"No, I can't. Ma says Da never planned for me to go to high school. She doesn't know if I can. I might have to get a job."

This is news to me. Mary, the smartest girl in her class, might not go to high school?

"Well, tell them you want to go to high school. You could do it. Look what happened when all those ladies marched around to get the right to vote. Look at Ma studying to be a nurse."

Mary's still quiet.

"Ain't you the top of your class?"

"Almost," she says.

"Well, then?" I say.

"I got a scholarship to St. Leo for a four-year academic degree, but Ma says I should just go to Nativity or St. Bridget for a two-year commercial degree. And maybe not even finish there."

"What's the difference?" I ask.

"Billy, don't you know anything? If I want to go to

college, I have to go to St. Leo. Everybody knows that." And she flounces her hair in her Big Bossy know-it-all-way. All this school talk gets me thinking I might need to start worrying about my future.

"Well, where do I have to go?"

"You'll go to De La Salle, no matter what." She points over toward Wabash Avenue. "But I can't go there, because it's only for boys." She hisses the end of boys, right in my face.

I say, "I don't want to go to high school. I'm going to play baseball."

"Well, isn't that nice?" Mary folds her arms over her chest.

Gol dang, what'd I say wrong? I can't help it I was born a boy, can I?

I don't know what to say to Mary. Do I got to cross the line for everybody these days? Then I think, *Do what you can, with what you've got, where you are.*

I hand Mary the stack of cards. "I'm going to tell Da how smart you are. And Ma will let you go to St. Leo. You'll see." Then I say my favorite line from the *Mutt and Jeff* comic strip I read. "Oowah! Easy come. Easy go."

Mary gives a little giggle and touches my arm. "Go to the beach, you little shyster."

Most of the sidewalks are empty of the folks going to Sunday Mass while I'm heading to Bubbly Creek. Timmy won't come for me until after Mass, so I'm safe, I think.

And what of it when he does? He don't own me. If I want to be friends with Foster then I will be, doggone it. It's going to be a great, great day, thanks to me and my great ideas. After we do a trial run with the raft, there's lots of summer left to fix what don't work. Lots of time to plan our real trip. Get our bedrolls ready and store up some supplies. To leave charged-up Chicago for cool Canada where we don't got to worry about that ever-lovin' line.

The woods have a stifling, sticky smell, as if the world's radiator cap's been letting steam out all night. All the buzzing and chirping and humming gets on my nerves. I feel jumpy. "Shut up already," I whisper to the woods.

Foster and Odell are down by the water when I come into the clearing. Emmett sits by the fire with his feet stretched out. "Billy!" Foster whoops when he sees me. "What're you doing here on a Sunday?"

"Getting some landlubbers on a boat!"

"All right!" says Foster. "We'll show Tom Sawyer and Huck Finn just how it's done."

"We ain't going nowhere," says Odell, and he puts his feet apart and folds his arms across his chest.

"Come on, Odell," I say. "We can leave the raft tied up. Let's just push her out and see if she floats."

So we stock the crate with three mason jars of fresh water and a folded-up tarp Emmett found at the factory. We put two sturdy oak poles, whittled smooth, into the crate. The plan is to stick them into the spaces between the boards and stretch the tarp over them like a tent for a canopy. Then we put one thicker pole on the raft for pushing us along. Me and Foster been conniving all along for what we might need on our maiden voyage.

"Hey, help me break this spiky part," Foster calls to me.

I come round the side of the raft where he's struggling with a pointed barb on the top of the pole.

"This might poke somebody by accident," he says and holds it out.

"Use your knife," I tell him. "Saw it off." And then I remember. His knife and his Buffalo nickel belong to some no-good Hamburg now. "Here, use mine," I say. And I toss him my pocketknife that I keep nice and sharp, just the way my da taught me.

"Look, Billy," Emmett says, and I glance over. A coffee can is sitting on the fire pit, and Emmett tilts it so I can see inside. Something brown and gooey oozes toward the edge.

"Eww. What is it?"

"Birch tar," he answers. "I saw this stuff dripping from a log we was burning. Daddy says birch tar is good for sealing up cracks."

Straight away we set to slathering that sticky mess in between all the logs and boards. We only have enough for about half the raft, but when Foster pours a cup of river water over it, the liquid beads up and runs right back where it came from.

The sun sparkles down on us and a dragonfly gets himself stuck to the fresh tar. *Poor guy*, I think. *Bet you never thought that would happen today, did you?* I take a stick and try to move him, but he beats his wings harder, just sticking himself in deeper. Finally, I scoop up the dragonfly and the whole glob of tar and throw it in the river, hoping the water will loosen the tar. I think again how life is unpredictable, even for dragonflies.

We push the raft out into the creek until it's just a few inches from the shore. It bobs a bit with the current. Then we get on, one by one. I'm the last, and I push the raft just slightly so we aren't scraping on the gravel banks.

For just a minute all is grand. We're afloat. Each of us in our own glorious position. Odell holds tight to the edge of the raft. Foster stands in the middle with his hand on the tarp poles. Emmett sits cross-legged, leaning his back on the crate. I'm standing like a warrior. Then suddenly I'm on all fours, trying to keep my balance as the raft is swept out into a current we never thought about.

The front tips and Odell's head goes under, then the whole side of the raft plunges under and hits the bottom of the creek. It bobs up and then everything starts all over as the raft, caught tight to its tether, can't right itself. I can feel it shuddering, begging to be free or break apart trying.

"Hang on," I yell.

I jump off and half swim, half run up the bank to the tree we tied the raft to. The tree is bent almost double with the weight of the raft. It's a sapling—maple, I think—with its little pointed-hand leaves making halos above my head. I shimmy the rope up to the midpoint of the tree and wrap my hand around the trunk to hold the little sapling steady.

"What're you doing, Billy?" The voice comes from behind me. Surprised, I turn to look into the woods.

Timmy stands on the path, the shadows of the trees and his black cap darkening his face.

He followed me? For a minute I'm confused, and then I see he's wearing his bathing suit and holding his towel. And I remember. The beach. He came to get me. He must have known I'd be here.

I stare at Timmy. Who is he, really? Who am I? So many moments flash by me. The first ones I picture are the bright, light-filled, best-friend Timmy moments:

Sledding breakneck down Nightmare Hill.

Sneaking into abandoned buildings to pretend we were pirates on Captain Kidd's ship.

Taking the trolley to the Loop and eating corned beef at the Berghoff with his da.

Sharing his Lincoln Logs with me, before he'd even opened up the packages.

Bringing me his best ringer when my baby brother died in the hospital.

Telling me his da would help me out when mine come home from war with shell shock.

I can easily say I'm playing a mean trick on Foster and his brothers, about to desert that no-good squatter family on the river. In my head, I hear Emmett saying, "Sometimes it's best to look the other way. Keep your head down and your mouth shut."

It's not too late to choose my friend Timmy and let Foster and his brothers find their own way out of the river. Timmy and I will laugh all the way to the beach at their misfortune and my wit. He'll tell Mickey and Joey what I done and everything will turn up trumps for me. I'll make points with them Hamburgs, and they'll keep my family safe during these hard times.

My thoughts move fast. Faster than light. And in a blink, new moments fall into my head like dominoes, dark and troublesome:

Timmy's bloody ear and Mrs. Beatty's black eye.

Timmy throwing the bricks at black wagon drivers.

Him and his da's mean talk while we're working on the docks.

The puppy and the bottle and him calling me that ugly name.

Foster hanging in the bathroom stall, his treasures all dumped out on the floor, his lip all bloody.

Timmy spying on me. Watching Mickey threaten me at the baseball field.

There's a choice to be made. Like in a shell game. The pea is under one of the walnut shells and I got to pick the right one. I hear my da and Mr. Williams telling me, "Do what you can, with what you've got, where you are."

What I can do is save my friends. What I have is just my good heart and my mouth. Where I am is here, right now. And if I don't do something then I'm the dis-en-fran-chise-ment Odell talks about. If I don't do something then I'm no better than Timmy and Mickey.

Oh, there's costs to be paid, all right. And either way, if I don't pay the costs, then risky, unpredictable, bad things might happen. But there ain't a middle ground anymore. Maybe there never was. If I ain't on one side, I'm on the other. If I ain't crossing the line, then I'm no better than those folks gawking at the lynchings.

In my head I see my drawing of our raft, BEST FRIENDS printed on the side in Foster's neat handwriting. I hear Da laughing for the first time since he went off to war. I smell Ma's scones and taste the tea she makes for me and I feel Anna hugging my neck and Mary touching my arm. *Under the shelter of each other, we survive.*

I stare back at Timmy through the branches of the baby maple tree. I know which shell to pick. I take a deep breath and say, "It don't have to be like this, you know. Come with us."

But when he growls back at me, it's in his da's surly voice. "You know what you are? You're a—"

I don't give him a chance to say it. "I know what I am. And I ain't no coward."

And when I say it, I realize how a boy's father gets a hold of him and don't let go, and I wish Timmy could of knowed my da better, instead of only his.

With a sudden crack, the sapling splinters, not quite

breaking clean in half. I quick yank the rope up over the fractured bit. I'm just trying to untangle it from the sad little tree, when it slithers away from me, tearing off leaves and small branches as it whips away.

I hear frantic voices coming from the raft. "Billy! Help!"

I hear my da in my own head. "Your heart knows your mind, Billy."

And just that fast I do what I know I have to do. I charge after the rope, and one second before it leaves the bank, I catch it and pull with all my might.

I hear Timmy yell out, "You're a double-crossing N—— lover, that's what."

Hard as I try I can't hold the raft. Now that it's free, the current is stronger than any of us imagined and the raft wants to careen on downstream.

"Jump off," I yell. And then, seeing the panic in their eyes, I remember. The Williams brothers can't swim.

The rope rips into the skin on my hands, and as I feel it slipping through them, my only hope is to run with it, into the water, and use it to guide me to the raft. I hurtle into the creek, splashing like a baby in the bath. And then I'm running, tripping, flailing, and half swimming, never letting go of that rope. It drags me under, water cascades into my eyes and over my head, and I have to hold my breath while I pull that rope inch by inch to bring me closer to the raft.

Hands pull me up. I lie on my back, gasping for breath.

And then I notice that even with four of us on it, the raft bobs along, barely taking any water over the edges. Incredible. We've built a real, honest-to-goodness raft. And I'm proud as pie. But now what?

Chapter Fourteen

I SIT UP, SMILING. THIS is the best thing that's happened all summer. Maybe the best thing ever. But when I turn to congratulate my fellow raft builders, Odell and Emmett are scowling, and Foster's eyes are bigger than a diner donut.

"Tarnation. What'd ya go and do that for? You untied us," says Odell.

"What were you thinking? How we gonna get back?" says Emmett.

"I was trying to save the raft," I say. "Keep it afloat. Then I couldn't hold it. What if I just let go? What then?" Gol dang. I go and save them, and they're mad at me.

"But, Billy, now we're stranded." Foster's voice is high and shaky.

With a sudden pang I realize they're more scared than mad. I guess I'd be scared, too, if I didn't know how to swim. I point back to the lean-to and the clearing. "Don't worry. We can just float to the calm water and paddle toward the shore. We'll pull the raft close and walk her back on the banks of the creek."

"The banks are steep down by the river. We won't be able to hold her."

Well, I hadn't thought of that. Walls of cement and metal keep the river from overflowing its banks. Then I remember the factory docks along the river. They come right up to the water to make it easy to load and unload barges full of supplies. "Okay, then, we'll pull her up alongside a dock and jump off."

Odell shakes his head. "No factory's gonna let us just dance over and climb up on their dock."

"Well, if we have to, we'll jump up on the wall and let her float to sea. Come on, Foster," I say, hoping to get him on my side. "We may as well have fun on our maiden voyage, especially if we might have to abandon her down the river."

Foster looks at me and then at the river. Then he grins,

lets loose his grip on the poles and sits down next to me. "It's real peaceful, ain't it, W. J. McDermott?"

I grin. "It sure is, F. J. Williams."

We dangle our feet over the edge of the raft and let the muddy water tickle our toes.

"There any snakes in this creek?"

"Nah. I never seen one."

His shoulders relax. "My Daddy's friend got hisself killed by a snake in Mississippi. A cottonmouth, right there in the river."

"No, it wasn't, you dummy," says Odell. "It was in the woods."

"No. Daddy told me he was fishing, so keep my eyes open."

"Daddy's friend was *going* fishing, walking through the cane field. It was a canebrake rattlesnake got him."

"Anyway, no snake's gonna swim up to the top of the water to bite your stinkin' feet," I tell Foster.

Foster splashes me, but it don't matter 'cause I'm still all wet from my raft rescue. I strip off my shirt and lay it out to dry. Everyone copies me and the sun beats down on us, melting the fear a bit.

Foster holds his arm up next to mine. "You're like a peeled potato in this here potato basket."

We all laugh. It's true—even Emmett with his lighter skin is shades darker than my pink-white chest. Just like when we were at the White Sox game, I wonder if dark skin gets sunburn. But I don't ask.

We settle down with two of us on each side of the raft for balance, Odell closer to the middle than the edge, and start to enjoy the ride. Emmett passes the jar of water around a few times, just the way I imagine Tom Sawyer and Huck Finn did on their raft. The river water reflects pinpricks of sunlight that dance in the ripples and the drag-onflies hover above us, shimmering like tiny, green fairies.

No one else notices when we pass a little point of land. No one but me and the big, gray bird standing on a low tree branch. His proud beak turns as his eyes follow the raft, and I can see the black feathers sticking out behind his head like a baseball cap on backwards.

Suddenly he takes off, the branch snapping up as his weight leaves it. His huge wings flap once and his long legs go straight as sticks. His enormous shadow sails right over the raft, and I think about flying dinosaurs and airplanes and blimps. And then I think about how small the raft feels and how wide the creek looks.

And that's when I realize what's happened. We shot right out of Bubbly Creek and into the Chicago River. We must be heading to Ohio, or maybe Indiana. I hope Ma doesn't think I'm running away. I guess we shoulda left a note.

But I keep tight-lipped about where we are. It won't do no good getting everybody upset.

The raft slows down until we're moving the same as a cottonwood seed on the breeze. It's peaceful. Quiet. I take my shirt, ball it up, and lay my head back on it. I see bluer-than-blue sky. I see wild areas along the banks and then the tassels of somebody's garden corn, standing soldier-like along the bank. I see the backs of factories and the pipes of the coal refinery, puffing more smoke than Mayor Thompson's cigar. And then we come up on a train bridge that looks like a giant pair of scissors fallen across the river, and I know the spell is broken.

"What's that, Billy? The Western Avenue Railroad Bridge?" asks Emmett.

"We're floating out too far. We'll never get back," says Odell.

"Come on," I say. "This is the Chicago River. It's about as safe as a bathtub. We can paddle back when we want." Truth be told, though, I ain't really sure about that. I never been this direction on the river. I been downriver, where it goes under the downtown bridges and out toward the lake. I been near the North Branch, by the entrance to

Riverview, with my da. But I ain't exactly sure what's this way—shallow marshy spots or roaring waterfalls.

"They changed the way the river flows, some years back," I tell the Williams boys.

"Nah, they didn't." Emmett thinks I'm joking.

"They did. They wanted to keep all the junk from going downstream, so now the river flows away from Chicago."

"How'd they do that?" Odell asks.

"I don't know. Bunch of engineers, I guess."

Odell studies the ripples in the water. "I'm going to be an engineer." He thinks for a long moment. "Maybe go back to Mississippi and do the same thing—keep the water from flowing into the ocean."

"Yeah?" Emmett says. "Well, Einstein, you ain't never even been to the ocean. How do you know they even want the Mississippi reversed?" He takes a pull from the mason jar and spits a stream of water at Odell.

"I know more than you, you lily-livered dropout." Odell grabs a tarp pole from the crate and hits the side of the raft, next to where Emmett is sitting.

I don't have a brother, but if I said those things to my sisters, Ma would skin me alive. It makes me nervous to see them fight. "Come on, let's try to paddle back to the creek," I say.

Foster and I lay flat and hang our arms over the end of the raft that's pointing toward Bubbly Creek. We paddle with our hands, but it's hard to tell if it makes a difference.

The banks are lower here, full of flowers, orange and blue. No factories. I look back the other way, the way we're floating, and I can see some private docks way up ahead. I start planning how we're going to head that way, jump on a dock and walk home. If only we could all swim. That old "if only" again.

"Billy," Foster's vice jolts me back to the present. "There's a dead tree. Let's see if we can get to it."

We paddle hard, and it's uncomfortable. The rough edges of the raft scrape my chest.

"Let's get on the sides and use one arm each like a paddle."

We experiment with lying and sitting and kneeling, urged on by Odell and Emmett. We finally decide we get the best whoosh when we kneel, hold the front of the raft with one hand, and paddle with the other.

"I ain't left-handed, Billy. This ain't working."

"Here, let me," says Emmett, and he scooches toward the edge.

Odell is still sitting in the middle of the raft. Still close to the Pride of the River crate. I scoop up some water and splash him.

He tenses and grabs onto the crate. "Cut it out," he yells. His bony knuckles reflect the sun rays.

"Want a turn?" I ask him while Emmett and Foster switch places.

"If you sissies can't manage," Odell says, but doesn't move a muscle.

Even with Emmett on the left, we don't seem to be getting closer to the dead tree. Might be getting farther away. It's hard to tell on the water. I rest my arm, trailing my hand over the side.

My white hand is brown in the water. Caramel. When the good Lord was making up people, how did he choose their color? The best thing about being in the middle of the river is there ain't nobody worrying about color out here.

Just when I have that thought, a noise comes out of nowhere. We all sit up and look at each other, then at the sky. Maybe a blimp. It's coming up too slow to be an airplane.

Foster points upriver, and we all look. Putt-putting around the bend is a boat that looks like a slice of an apple from so far off. We watch as it comes closer, the pointed bow cutting through the water. A roof of canvas covers part of the boat. A tall man in overalls stands in the front and steers, and a short, fat man holds on to the side. I can smell his pipe before I can see it.

Our little raft tips back and forth as the motorboat comes alongside us. Odell wraps his free arm around his knees.

"It's Mutt and Jeff," I whisper to Foster.

"Who?"

"Mutt and Jeff, from the comic strip. You know, the tall guy and the fat guy."

Foster shakes his head. "I don't know no Mutt and Jeff."

The motor cuts to idle and the boat glides closer.

"Hey boys," the fat man calls out to us.

"Hey," I yell back.

"What're you doing out here?" He looks right at me when he asks. I know he's wondering how a white boy come to be riding on a raft with three black boys, out in the middle of the Chicago River.

"It's a school project. We're acting out Tom Sawyer and Huck Finn," I say, and I hear Foster cough.

The man nods, approving of my answer. "Nice raft," he says.

"Thanks."

"Where you heading?"

I know I been striking out lately in the character-judgment department. First, I believed Mickey was my chum. Second, I mistook Mr. Weinstein for a spy. And third, I held out for Timmy to change his mind. But Mutt and Jeff sure do have friendly faces. They seem just like the sort of folk my da would be joining for a pint.

I take a closer look at their boat. A polished wooden box is built into the middle of the boat, maybe to hide the engine. Slots at the back hold a couple of fishing poles. And open on the floor is a satchel with a bottle of whiskey in it. They're just a couple of fishermen relaxing on a Sunday afternoon. Harmless as candy.

I make up my mind and say, "We're heading back that way." I point where Bubbly Creek intersects with the river.

"Throw us your line and we'll give you a tow." The fat man taps the bowl of his pipe into his hand and tosses the ashes into the river.

"No, Billy. Don't." Odell hasn't moved. "They'll go too fast. We'll tip over."

"We can untie ourselves if we want," I argue.

"We ain't making progress paddling, Odell, you can see that," Emmett says. "Billy's right. We'll just loose the cable if we need to."

Foster pulls the cable with the rope up out of the water, and we maneuver the Pride of the River behind the fishermen.

First I toss the cable at the boat, but it falls short, and the raft sways with my movement. Then Foster tries. It's closer this time, but the fat man can't reach the rope before it sinks down into the river.

The tall man leaves the steering wheel and comes to the back. His dark hair peeks out from under his white boating cap. I wouldn't be surprised if he's got some loot, from the way he looks. When Emmett throws the cable, his long arm reaches out and snatches the rope end, just the way Shoeless Joe goes up and saves a run. He hands it to the fat man.

"Tie it to the cleat at the bottom of the transom," he says.

So the fat man ties the rope through a metal bar at the bottom of the boat's flat rear wall, just under the fancy gold lettering declaring the boat's name: HARPER'S FERRY.

"Hang tight, sailors," calls the tall man, and waves.

The fat man hands him the bottle and the golden liquor shines as he takes a long drink. The fat man turns and grins at us, and then with a growl from the engine, we're moving forward.

"Yee-haw!" I whoop.

Foster yells, "Give it the green!" and I laugh.

We put our hands in the water and it dances up and

over them, making little waterfalls down our wrists. The front of the raft tilts up where the cable is attached to it. We all lie flat on our stomachs and hang on so we don't fall off backwards. I close my eyes and imagine I'm on the Shoot the Chute ride at Riverview Park, picking up speed right before plunging into the water.

Mutt and Jeff go slow and steady, and we all relax. Well, all of us but scaredy-cat Odell, who keeps his hands in a tight grip on the cable.

It's hard to tell how much time has passed since we first pushed the raft off the gravelly shore of Bubbly Creek. I think about Tom Sawyer and Huck Finn, away from home for days on their raft, and my stomach gets a funny ache—a cross between happiness and homesickness, making me feel right silly.

The sun beats hot on our heads, but the water and the wind cool us off. The riverbanks fly by like a moving picture show, and I'm seeing the whole scene blending together now, all the trees and plants going by in a swirl of colors.

"Think they're rich?" I ask, nodding to the boaters.

"Oh, they got lots of mazuma, all right," says Emmett.

"Mazuma?" Foster laughs. "Where'd you get that word?"

"Picking up rubbish over on Maxwell. That's what they say about the store owners."

"Did you see the wristwatch on the tall one?" asks Odell.

"Maybe he was an officer in the war," I say. "All the officers wore watches. Trench watches." I'm an expert on this on account of Timmy's da telling Timmy all about war stuff, and then him telling me.

"You sure know your onions, Billy, don't you?" says Odell, making fun of me. "Maybe he was a general, even." He lets go with one of his hands and pokes me in the ribs.

"Go soak your head," I tell him. "What do you think the name means?" I point to the gold-lettered HARPER'S FERRY.

"Maybe the guy's name is Harper and it's his ferry," says Foster.

"Maybe it's named after a real ferry boat," says Emmett.

Odell pipes up, "Or maybe he's from Virginia. Harper's Ferry is a town there."

"How do you know? You ain't never been to Virginia," says Emmett.

"'Member that song, 'John Brown's Body'?"

"No," me and Foster say right at the same time.

Odell starts singing and Emmett joins in:

John Brown's body lies a-mouldering in the grave.

John Brown's body lies a-mouldering in the grave.
John Brown's body lies a-mouldering in the grave.
But his soul is marching on.

He captured Harper's Ferry with his nineteen men so few.

Me and Foster chime in, now that we know the song.

He captured Harper's Ferry with his nineteen men so few.
He captured Harper's Ferry with his nineteen men so few.
But his soul is marching on.

And soon throughout the Sunny South the slaves'll all be free.
And soon throughout the Sunny South the slaves'll all be free.
And soon throughout the Sunny South the slaves'll all be free.
But his soul is marching on.

We're all in long pants, and melting from the sun. Emmett is the first to roll up his pant legs. I start to roll mine up, but slow-like, embarrassed of my two chalk-white legs.

Odell points at my legs and says, "He was white, you know. John Brown. A white man fighting for the slaves."

"Prolly the only one," I say.

"Probably," he says.

"I never heard about that before," I say. "I heard about Frederick Douglass."

He rolls up the legs of his pants and I see the scars on his legs. It makes me sorry for thinking he's a scaredy-cat.

"You ever hear about Harriet Tubman or William Carney?" asks Emmett.

I feel right ignorant. "No," I say.

Foster pipes up. "Yes, we did. In school. Maybe you wasn't there yet. Harriet Tubman made nineteen trips between the North and South. She helped three hundred slaves make it to freedom."

"That's something, especially for a woman," I say. Then I realize that I sound just like my da and Mr. Beatty, making me feel uncomfortable. Especially after my promise to Mary.

"And William Carney, he escaped from being a slave, joined up in the Civil War, and got hisself a Congressional Medal of Honor," continues Foster.

Foster sure remembers his history lessons. It almost makes me want to study a little harder. Almost.

"So, Billy," Odell says. "We ain't landlubbers anymore. You happy?"

"Tell us a story," I say. "A landlubber story."

Odell pulls himself around to the front of the crate,

knees bent, bracing his bare feet against one of the flat sitting boards. We crowd over alongside him, Emmett lying on his back, arms crossed behind his head, holding to the edge, eyes closed. *Next time*, I think, *we should put some rope handles for hanging on.*

Odell squeezes his hands together, right over left, then left over right. He looks at the riverbanks, then at the river, and then at us. It's easy to see that tall, strong Odell would rather be safe on shore. "I don't think I got a story today, Fozzy. You got to do it."

"Me? I can't tell stories. Emmett? Billy?"

Emmett opens one eye, but doesn't answer. I'm not a storyteller like Odell, or even as good as Mary. But maybe telling a story is my penance for being to blame for this river adventure. And it would be a shame to waste the whole trip without a story, wouldn't it? The dragonflies reminded me of this story, back when we were heading the other way up the river.

"I don't know any landlubber stories," I say. "But I remember a ghost story."

Emmett lifts his head. "I'd listen to a ghost story. But Fozzy might get scared."

"Will not," says Foster, and flicks at Emmett's bare leg with his finger.

Odell moves over, keeping a grip on the crate, and I take his place. It's not easy to start a story, I realize, and I take a deep breath.

"Well, a brand-new theater opened in Chicago in 1903. The Iroquois Theater. It was so beautiful. More beautiful than the most beautiful thing in Chicago. The builders rushed to get it done because a special Christmas show was coming to town, 'Mr. Bluebeard,' and everybody wanted to see it."

"Bluebeard? Like the pirate?" says Foster.

"No, that's Blackbeard the pirate, Beechnut," says Emmett.

Foster flicks Emmett again. "Did you go see it, Billy?" says Foster.

"No, I wasn't born yet."

"Did your ma and da go see it?"

"Fozzy, stop interrupting the story," says Odell.

I glare at Fozzy. "No, they were still in Ireland. You want me to tell it, or not?"

Fozzy pipes down. I pull myself up and stand, partly propped on the crate. I'm new at this storytelling. A little nervous. But my audience waits and the hum of the motorboat cues me on.

"Anyway, so on the day of the matinee, one day before New Year's Eve, the crowd packs into the theater. They say over two thousand people come to see it, with lots of kids since they were off school for the break. Just when the second act comes on some sparks start a little fire, and people start to get riled."

"Is this the Chicago Fire?" Foster butts in. "We heard about that. A cow started that."

"That ain't this story. But that ain't true, anyway. You want me to tell this story?" Gol dang but it's hard to tell a story with people butting in.

"Don't mind him, Billy," says Emmett.

"Okay, so the thing is, after the Chicago Fire they made all kinds of new laws for buildings but the builders didn't follow the laws when they built the Iroquois because they were in such a hurry to get the building done. No fire curtain, no fire extinguishers, no emergency lighting, no fire escape, no roof vents, nothing, on account of Bluebeard coming to town."

My da tells this story to us on New Year's Eve. And Mary told it while he's been gone. I start to worry I won't tell it right.

"Keep going, Billy," says Odell, relaxing his grip on the crate and stretching out his arms.

"Okay, so anyway, the sparks didn't look too bad, and the main actor told one of the crew to get a fire extinguisher and put it out. He told the audience not to worry and they started up the music. That got the people paying attention and they forgot about the fire and went back to watching the show. The exciting part was coming and nobody wanted to miss it."

"What was the exciting part, Billy?" Foster's eyes are round.

"A fairy, dressed in green, waited behind the curtain to fly out over the audience on a wire and sprinkle them with pink carnations. Everybody who'd been to the show said that was their favorite part. Well, the crewman came back without a fire extinguisher, because there weren't any new ones, but an actor found an old-fashioned fire extinguisher—the kind with the chemical powder in it—so they tried throwing the powder on the fire. But it only made the fire worse. And just about that time somebody opened a back exit and a gust of wind shot right up to the sparks, making a fireball that flew into the audience, starting everything burning."

Foster interrupts. "Is this a ghost story or a fire story, Billy?"

"Shh. Let him tell it," says Emmett.

Their eyes are all staring at me and I feel like I'm casting a spell. I continue, a little slower, with more breath in my voice for effect. "The people all jumped up to get out but they couldn't see the doors because the emergency lighting wasn't put in. The people that did find the doors couldn't get them open because the crowd was pushing against them, holding them shut. The audience in the second and third balcony ran for the fire escape but the builders hadn't put them on the building, and so they jumped out the fire escape doors and died."

I stop to lick my lips, and stand all the way straight, giving my back a rest.

"That's awful, just awful," whispers Odell.

"Yah. Yah, it was. The bodies piled up ten deep and Marshall Field, you know, the man who owns Marshall Field's, stopped doing business and told everybody to carry the linens from his store across the street to cover up the six hundred poor dead souls lying in the alley—what they now call Death Alley. Chicago didn't even celebrate New Year's Eve in 1903, on account of the sadness over all the dead."

"What happened to the Green Fairy?" Foster asks, just like I been waiting for him to do.

I look around at my three friends. Their faces are not moving. In fact, it looks like they're not breathing.

"We-ell." I draw out the word. I pause. "The Green Fairy was never seen again. Almost all of the actors got out. But not the Green Fairy. People say"—I make my voice go low and haunted—"if you go down Death Alley late at night, where they laid all the bodies, you'll see the Green Fairy fly overhead with her basket of pink carnations. And if you're lucky she'll toss one to you."

At this, I put my hand up and pretend to toss a flower, but that's when I notice we're about to pass under a bridge—a lift bridge that I recognize. I give out a gasp.

"What?" asks Emmett.

I stand up and point to the river behind us. While I was telling the story we left Bubbly Creek and Bridgeport far behind. Near as I can figure, we're now coming up to the Van Buren Street Bridge. They put a tunnel right close to here for the cable cars to go under the river. I smell factories instead of fish, and I see filmy rainbows from boat oil mucking up the water. And I hear a train whistle.

Suddenly the engine of Harper's Ferry throttles down, and I lose my balance and tumble back as our speed goes from Shoot-the-Chute fast to merry-go-round slow.

I point toward our towboat, where Mutt and Jeff are barely visible. They're slumped down in the seats with their feet propped up on the bow, nodding off.

The skyline of Chicago looms in front of us. I'm jumpy as a jitterbug. Excited and worried at the same time. And a little embarrassed, too, remembering my big boast that getting back was easy as pie.

This is a real adventure to tell about, danger and all. *Boy, oh boy!* I think.

Chapter Fifteen

"What is it, Billy?" asks Foster.

"Look where we are. Right here near downtown. Look." I wave my arms at the buildings.

Odell and Emmett sit straight up, their eyes roaming over the riverbanks.

"What happened? Did they forget about us?" asks Emmett.

"I don't know, but we should yell for them to untie us. It will take all day to drift back home."

So we yell, and holler, and scream. But too many boats and cars and trains and machines are making more noise than us.

Gray concrete walls and wooden landings have replaced the green of the riverbanks. We even pass a cruise ship docked next to a hotel.

It reminds me of the *Eastland* Disaster, the cruise ship that tipped over in the river in 1915. I tell them all about it, enjoying my power as a storyteller to shock my listeners.

"They was going for a picnic to Indiana. Just a picnic, but the boat was so heavy, and too many passengers were standing on the deck, so it started to tip. The water came rushing in it and it tipped all the way. The passengers climbed out the windows and walked on the hull of the ship to the dock. Except for the ones who died."

"How many died?" asks Odell.

"Eight hundred forty-four died, and fifty-eight of them was babies. Can you imagine? There was 2,500 on the boat so they rescued more than half, but still, what with that boat being only twenty feet from the wharf, you'd think those 844 people shoulda made it, too," I say, shaking my head. All our eyes are on the water, imagining all those poor people. "My da saw it in the paper, so he took me to see that sorry boat lying on its side in the water, before they heaved it upright."

I remember that day, clear as a bell. I was seven. Only seven years old. But all the same, I felt a hole in my heart for those dead people, wishing I could of done something to save them from drowning. We stood there, me and Da, his hand on my shoulder. Quiet and still, respecting the dead, awed at the size of the boat—like a building collapsed in the river. That was before my da went off to the war, when so many other things around me collapsed like that boat.

"Oh, Lordy. Hope that one don't tip over," Odell says and edges away from the massive black hull.

Then we see the passengers on the cruise ship noticing us, and we all let out a yell, waving our arms to get their attention. The other boaters think we're waving at them and they smile and hold up their hands. Pretty girls with pretty scarves blow kisses to Odell, and I can see him fighting an embarrassed grin over his tight-clenched teeth.

Mutt and Jeff's boat jerks, swerving wildly.

"They're trying to kill us!" Odell wails.

"No, they're tanked," Emmett says. "Pickled drunk. They're trying not to hit anything." Emmett turns to me. "Billy, we've got to untie ourselves." And he slides up to the front and wrestles with the cable.

I guess it just shows we're landlubbers, all right, because we never figured that the pressure from Harper's Ferry pulling would take up the slack and tighten the knot, making it impossible for us to get loose.

"We got to cut it," says Emmett. "Foster, you got your knife?"

Foster digs in his pocket and fishes out his treasure pouch. He hands my knife to me and says, "I didn't get a chance to give it back before the raft went wild."

I shake my head. "Keep it. For our next trip. I'll ask my da for his old one."

Foster says, "Thanks, Billy," and gives the knife to Emmett.

"No, you cut," Emmett says. "I'll hold it still."

When we attached the cable to the raft, we wrapped it around the crossbar that was holding the telephone poles in line, then banded it together with wire and twine, only leaving about a foot between the raft and the end of the cable. And then we poured a good amount of that home-made birch tar all over it. Emmett lies flat on his stomach and holds the cable clear of the water while Foster saws at it.

Odell and I keep balance and watch as the raft floats into the mouth of the city. We're like Lewis and Clark entering a tall canyon, the blue sky a ribbon above us. The buildings tower over us like an open-roofed tunnel, their reflections rippling on the currents. The roar from the bridge traffic echoes between the banks, the sound of a lion prowling.

Next to the tall buildings, great barges, and ships, the raft is nothing—just a pile of debris, easily smashed to bits with one wrong turn. A loud creak jolts us and the rolling lift bridge ahead splits in the middle and rises toward the sky, opening up a water lane for a tall ship. We're so close. If we were taller, we could grab hold of its steel trusses and hoist ourselves free of our floating trap.

But in no time the bridge is behind us and I glance at Foster's progress. He's managed to fray a few pieces of the cable, but his hands are getting so sticky with tar that he can't hardly maneuver the knife and he steadies himself by curling his leg around the side of the raft, leaning out over the water.

And then suddenly I don't see him. Emmett drops the cable. I jump up and grab one of the poles.

"Foster," I scream, searching the water.

His head comes up and he's flapping his arms, coughing out water.

"Help! Help!" he wails before he goes under.

Odell stands up and the raft wobbles.

I hold out the pole, but when he surfaces again Foster can't reach it. Every second, we're moving away from him.

I'm about to jump in after him when Odell throws out the tarp, keeping hold of one end. It fans out in front of Foster's arms and he grabs for it.

"Help me," Odell says, straining to hold the tarp.

I let loose of the pole and we heave, pulling Foster closer, struggling against the speed of the boat. When he's close enough, I lean over the side and grab under his arms, helping him pull himself up.

I ain't never heard Foster say one swear word. Not one. So I don't blame him for what he says as he splays himself out on the raft, shuddering through his whole body.

Odell sinks down to his knees, clasping Foster's shoulder with a wild look in his eyes.

When we're sure Foster's safe, Emmett says, "Billy, take a look at this." He motions me toward the front.

The cable is holding fast on account of our great wiring job and the tar we poured over it, but the front board, the one right behind the cable, is loose.

I test the board with my foot. "Think we could jimmy it off? And if we do, can we make it to the river bank in time before we're out in the lake?"

"What lake?" Odell asks. His voice has a quiver in it that don't seem to be caused by the motion of the boat.

Don't he know? Don't everybody know? Where else would the Chicago River go? "Lake Michigan," I say.

But there's no time to explain now. Every second we're moving closer and closer to that lake, and we got to do something fast. The broad band of the river blends into the wide, gray body of water with no more than a color shade of change to show the difference.

Emmett and I grab hold of the sides of the raft and kick at the board attached to the cable with all our might. Just as we float under the State Street Bridge the board gives way and the cable, board still dangling off its end, dances off after Harper's Ferry.

We're free and we're suddenly sideways, unbalanced and bobbing, heading for the canal wall.

"Get the pole. Push us off the wall," I yell.

Foster is still flat on his back, so Odell reaches for the pole and manages to jam it into the wall just in time, before we crash. A dozen seagulls scold us and whoosh away from their perches on the wall, circling above our heads. Odell ducks as one comes mighty close to him, squawking its warning.

If we can just keep to the edge, maybe we can creep back along the river using the slight current from the change in the river flow. But we're battered by the wake of every speedboat passing us, all of them heading for a cool cruise on this hot Sunday, their merry voices echoing over the water even as we fight for our lives. Me knowing it's all my fault.

"Hold the wall, can you?" I shout above the waves slapping and the gulls barking and the boats roaring.

Odell and I try to pull the raft back up the river using the flats of our hands against the wall, but it's no use. The cement is slimy with algae, green scummy stuff that slips across our palms.

I try to stand on the edge of the raft to reach the top of the wall, where it's drier, but the raft dips and I see everyone start to slide toward me. Emmett screams, "Billy!"

I sit back down and give up. There's nothing to do. It's hopeless. We're going to die, stranded in the middle of the lake. And it's my fault.

No one even knows where we are. No one will even know our names when our bodies wash up on shore. I hope Timmy feels sorry when he sees the missing person notice. I get a tear in my eye when I think about Ma at my funeral. I must have heatstroke, making me soft in the head.

At the end of the canal wall the waves chop and wallop the cement piers, just waiting to swallow us. There's nothing to do but hold on for dear life as we meet the lake. Like leeches on the river bottom, we press our whole bodies against the raft.

As we let go the protection of the wall and head into the lake, for just one tiny moment, my skin tingles and I feel touched by something magic. Good or bad, I don't know. Then it passes. The first wave washes over us and the left side of the raft angles up toward the sky.

"Paddle," I yell. "We gotta turn."

We row with our hands, the wood edges of the raft scraping against the undersides of our arms, the waves lapping up over the sides. We paddle and paddle and paddle, our muscles hot, with the cold waves trickling between our bodies and the boards. *Baked Alaska*, I think. That fancy ice cream dessert in Ma's *Cooking-School Cook Book* by Fannie Farmer. Ma told me all about it. Cold ice cream with a hot cookie around it.

All our paddling is working; our Baked Alaska raft is turning as it heads away from the river, inch by inch. We're past the breaking waves and leaving the busy Chicago Harbor. Rolls of water rock us as they push toward the shore, and I know we need to get stable if we're going to stay right side up.

"Come on, sit up," I say. "We got to balance."

Slowly we all bring our legs up pretzel style and sit. We sway and bob, but less water slops up over the sides. I scan the shore to get my bearings. Behind us and growing smaller is the Municipal Pier jutting way out into Lake Michigan. Someday I'm going to take my whole family there and buy everyone ice cream, stand on the upper deck, and watch the people. Someday, that is, if I'm not about to end up at my own funeral.

Looking the other way, the way we're being blown, I can see buildings in the background, like blocks stacked on end. And I know we're going the way we need to go. The pinpricks of reflected light are gone, transformed into glowing beams that ride the waves. I wonder what time it is. My face is drying, tight and prickly, in the breeze. Another sunburn, I'll wager.

"Okay," Emmett says. "Think we can paddle down toward a beach and then head into the shore?"

Odell twists his arm around and I see his scrapes are raw and bleeding. Foster and Emmett and me are scraped, too, but not like Odell. "Gol dang, Odell. Lean out more when you paddle," I say.

"I don't want to fall in. It's deep, ain't it?"

"Then put your shirt back on."

Emmett reaches into the crate and throws Odell his shirt. Then he passes us the jar of water. We haven't had time to drink any water in a while, and it tastes so good. I think how strange it is: water all around us and now water inside.

Then Emmett digs in the box and pulls out a jar I didn't

notice before. He takes a package out of the jar and unwraps the brown paper. Baby white eggs spill from the paper. Emmett pops one into his mouth and crunches down on it. He grins.

"I'll be gol danged," says Odell, giving me a jab to let me know he's making fun of my gol danging everything.

Emmett holds out the nest of white eggs to me.

"What is it?" I squint and try to steady my bobbing head to get a good look.

"Confetti."

"Nah. It's not." I gingerly pick up a white egg. It's the size of a marble, and stone-smooth.

"Yep. Did a rubbish pickup on Taylor for a truck that broke down. Owner of the Pompei restaurant came out and give us each a package. 'Grazie, grazie,' he says. 'Big wedding today. No need stink.'"

I put the smooth stone in my mouth. The white coating is candy sweet and when I bite it there's a loud crunch and I taste nut inside.

"What is it?" I ask again, reaching out my hand for another.

Emmett hands me one. "They call it confetti, or sometimes Jordan almonds. It's an Italian wedding thing. It's supposed to mean you'll have a sweet life together, even when the bitter, hard things happen."

I don't say anything. I think about my ma and da. All

248

the bitter and hard things that have happened. It doesn't seem sweet. I think about Mary and her secret under the stairs. That doesn't seem so sweet either. And the Williams brothers. All their troubles, living on the banks of Bubbly Creek, and Foster missing his ma.

Foster pokes my sunburned arm, holding half a nut. "Look, Billy. Maybe it's what happened to you. You was brown and got dipped in white. Maybe once all that pink blisters over and peels off, you'll be back to normal."

I go to poke him back. He laughs and moves as far from me as he can without falling back into the lake.

"Cut it out, you two." Odell still eyes the water, sitting like a ball, his arms wrapped so tightly around his knees that his fingers almost touch in the back.

We're bobbing with each ripple of the water, but there are no more angry waves. It's like Ma rocking Anna after a good scolding. We've drifted a fair ways from the mouth of the river. Pulled out by the invisible undertow, or blown by the wind? I don't know. The sun is hot. The wind is cool. The water is chill.

We are so small.

"Okay," I say. "Let's try to get to the beach. If we can get close to the breakwater, maybe we can pull up against it and climb off."

"What's a breakwater?" Emmett asks.

"You know, the rocks and cement they pile up so the waves don't come into the beach area." I point down the shoreline, where a skinny line of tan runs along the water. I know that's the breakwater, even though I can't see it. Most of the beaches have one. At least, I think they do. And surely lifeguards or rowboaters will see us and rescue us.

Even though it's taken God a precious long time to answer my prayers for my da, I say one for us to make it to the beach.

Chapter Sixteen

Emmett passes around the rest of the almonds and the last mason jar of water. "You know, we could all paddle from the front if it weren't for this crate being in the way."

"Okay," I say, knowing what he's thinking. I grab my shirt out of the crate and carefully pull it over my sun-burned back. Foster and Emmett pull theirs on, too.

Then Emmett rocks the crate back and forth, back and forth, until it finally comes loose. He pries it the rest of the way off with the tarp pole and gently sets our crate in the water with the empty mason jars inside. It floats away from us, dipping and twirling, like that famous carrier pigeon, Cher Ami, from the Great War. I remember reading how that bird flew through enemy fire and saved two hundred lives when it carried the message of the soldiers' location.

But then a swell of water tips our crate and our little carrier is gone.

"Gol dang," I whisper to myself.

"Pride of the River," Foster says.

We all lay facing the direction of the breakwater. Emmett and Odell on the outside, and me and Foster together in the middle. We lay flat as a pancake, but with our chests out over the edge, and paddle as if the gates of hell are open and the devil is chasing us. And it works. Along with the wind and the waves and our eight strong arms, we can see the rocks getting closer, little by little.

We take turns resting, the sun beating down and the cold water sluicing up to our chins. We're close enough now to see the shoreline, and we're passing by the first beach as we struggle to paddle nearer.

We angle in closer to the next beach, this one with a breakwater at its edge, and men fishing from up on top of it. To the left of the piles of rocks, farther in, I can see the sand, and it's jam packed with people, like pickles in a pickle jar.

"Should we try for the beach or the rocks?" I ask.

"Rocks," Emmett gasps. He's breathing hard, doing more work than the rest of us.

Then a thought comes to me, while I dangle my sore arms in the water: this very well might be the beach my family goes to.

A feeling of fear nags at me, and I wrestle it around in my head. I'm afraid for Foster and his brothers on account of their skin not being the same as mine. On account of the fact that I ain't never seen a dark-skinned beachgoer on this beach.

Will we be allowed to land? We don't have enough muscles left to paddle against the strength of Lake Michigan. Will people see that we're desperate? Desperate for our lives? Surely that will make a difference, won't it? Surely, people are kindhearted in the end, aren't they?

I remember Timmy blaming terror cars on blacks when *The Chicago Defender* said it was carloads of white sailors in Washington, DC, that killed six and wounded a hundred blacks. I remember Odell's scars from a white man's pitchfork and Emmett's fear haunting him all the time. I remember that awful feeling when I found Foster hanging in the bathroom and I couldn't do anything about it.

But I'm here now. Surely that will make a difference, won't it?

"Odell," I say.

He grunts at me, still paddling.

I lean up on one elbow. "I think we have to go back to the last beach. This beach might not be safe."

"What?" He goes still and looks at me. His voice is loud and angry.

"I don't know for sure. I'm just, it's just, it might . . ." I can't say it. I can't say, "This beach is for whites only." This is Chicago, not Mississippi. This is the North, not the segregated South.

Emmett hears us. "You mean there's a color line?" he asks. "Some beaches are for whites and some for blacks?"

I nod. Here we are, close enough to be rescued, and we could be in worse danger than being shipwrecked. I never took it serious before. I never had to. My pink-skinned life has always been fine and dandy. But I got to worry about more than me, myself, and I now. I got to worry about all of us.

Our country should be ashamed for allowing this. Our president should be ashamed he's ignored so much injustice. I'm ashamed I only started paying attention when it affected me. Just now, when I stand to lose something—my friends, my family, maybe my life.

Nobody's paddling now. We're all thinking of what to do.

"Okay," says Emmett. "Let's keep paddling, but once we get closer to the rocks, we'll turn the raft back to the last beach. I think it'll be easier when the water isn't so rough."

Everyone's quiet for a minute. Then Foster says, "I'm starving."

I look over at him. My stomach rumbles just thinking about what he said. "Me, too. What should we paddle for?"

"Fried chicken."

"Okay, twenty paddles for fried chicken." We laugh and paddle.

"Your turn," Foster says.

"Oyster stew. You ever been to the parish fair?"

"Nope."

"It's next week. We should go. There's a shooting gallery and a raffle. You can buy stuff. And oyster stew." Thinking about the parish fair makes me homesick for my ma and da.

"Yeah. Sure. Thirty for oyster stew at the parish fair," Foster says.

But who are we kidding? I'm talking to Foster, not Timmy. He can't go, just the same as I can't go eat fried chicken at his auntie's house. It makes me so mad I paddle forty 'stead of thirty.

"What else?" I say.

"Barbecue," Odell chimes in.

"Barbecue what?" I ask.

"You know. Just barbecue. Pit barbecue. They put the pig in the ground, cover it up with charcoal and wood, and smoke it all day. And that sweet sauce. Oh, Lord, don't it taste good?" Odell smacks his lips.

"I don't know. Ain't never had barbecue. How many strokes is it worth?" I ask.

"A hundred!"

We groan.

"Only if we add in poke salad and biscuits," says Emmett.

And we paddle. Me wondering what's poke salad and thinking biscuits don't taste as good as fresh-baked scones with a little cream and jam.

Soon we can see the faces of the people standing on the breakwater rocks. One man has a bottle in one hand and a fishing pole in the other. A girl and her fellow are holding hands, their legs dangling in the water. Three teenagers are aiming rocks at a buoy. A million people dot the beach— least that's what it looks like, all of them swarming in and out of the water.

I think about how I'm supposed to be at this beach, anyway. The Twenty-Ninth Street Beach. So, when we get off this raft, I can find Timmy and his da. Say I came looking for them. Say I been here all the time. Ma will be none the wiser and I'll be okay.

Then another thought: what if Timmy's da sees me on the raft with Foster? He'll know for sure I been lying. And what about my family? Will Mickey find out? "There's going to be hell to pay," he said. "There's going to be trouble." It haunts me. Who's going to pay? What trouble?

I hear my da. "Under the shelter of each other, we survive. We depend on each other. Promise me, you'll not judge a book by its cover."

Well, Da ain't here. Just me. To be the man. To protect the family. Well then, Da, I ain't no coward. Let 'em try to start something.

"Okay, we're close enough. Turn the raft to the other beach," Emmett shouts out. "Turn it."

But the raft has a mind of its own. It steers us closer to the breakwater rocks, no matter how hard we paddle against it.

Emmett sits up. "Foster, you and Odell stay down. Me and Billy will yell out."

At first I don't get it. Wouldn't it be better for us all to shout for help? To make a racket so they hear us over the hubbub? And then it hits me. Foster and Odell are dark, but me and Emmett are light. If they stay down, maybe no one will notice until we're safe on the shore.

"Are you sure?" sings out Foster.

"Darn sure, Fozzy," says Emmett. "In the South we got signs, Colored and White. In Chicago, there ain't no signs telling us where to go. You just gotta know."

I point a little farther down the shoreline. "If we can make it over there, you'll be okay." I pause. I'm embarrassed to ask, but I gotta know. "What about me? If we make it over there, will I be okay? A white boy on a black beach?"

Emmett lets out a hoot. "'Course you will. You ever hear tell of a white boy can't cross the colored line?"

"'Course, we don't know about pink boys, do we Emmett?" asks Odell, pointing to my sunburned arms.

"Oh, you're funny," I say.

"Funny lookin'," says Foster.

Just then I look up and see more people congregating on the breakwater. Maybe they see us, know we're in trouble, and are getting ready to help. One of the boys on the breakwater shouts. "Get on over here."

Or maybe he says, "Get on outta here." I can't hear him for sure. But we're so close I could jump off, swim and pull the raft behind me.

My mouth is open to ask Emmett if I should, when Odell screams, "Get down, Fozzy."

He pushes himself up with his arms and shoves Fozzy

and me down onto the raft. A rock the size of my fist crashes into his head.

It happens so fast, just like everybody always says. But it does. It happens so fast. One minute my mouth is open and the next I'm flat on the raft.

Odell topples over and falls off. Foster and I grab for him. Emmett throws him the poles. Odell's arms are pounding the water, trying to keep himself afloat. And the fear in his eyes as his head dips under is powerful awful to see.

"Kick your legs," I shout. "Move your arms like this." I make windmill motions. But we're drifting away from him and he's getting lost in the waves.

And the rocks keep coming. Splashing. Bouncing off the raft. Hitting us. Hitting Odell. There's loud shouts, and swearing.

"Get outta here." I hear it again and this time I understand. This time there's something in the voice—something I think I recognize—and it makes me look up at the breakwater, where for one second I'm positive I see Mr. Beatty, his pitching arm ready with another rock.

"Paddle. Hard," Emmett yells.

"No, don't leave him." I grab Emmett's arms.

"We'll run back to him." Emmett's voice catches. "The raft can't save him."

We paddle. As if life depends on it. And it does; Odell's life does. I keep looking back. People are leaving the break-water. I don't see Mr. Beatty. Was it really him? At first I'm sure I see Odell's head popping up between the waves, and then I ain't sure. Foster is crying but no sounds are coming out, just tears.

I shudder. That man meant to hit Foster with that rock, and maybe me, too. I just know it. To punish him for being friends with me. But it's not anybody's fault but mine. I'm the one who didn't follow the rules. I'm the one who made this happen. And Odell made the rock miss Foster, so it hit him instead. It's not fair. It's just not fair.

My eyes get wet. He'll be okay, I tell myself. He's strong and big. And more a hero than I'll ever be.

Our panicked paddling brings the raft quicker than ever to the black beach at Twenty-Fifth Street, and as soon as we get to water shallow enough that people are standing up, we jump off and feel the lake bottom with our feet.

We made it. We're safe. But there's no relief in saving ourselves now that we're frantic to get to Odell. Emmett shouts to a lifeguard, "My brother. He's drowning. Over there."

The lifeguard propels his rowboat to shore and sprints out ahead of us, motioning for others to help.

We run through the water, using our arms like shovels to propel us faster, until we're up on the beach. The heat smacks us in the face. The sand is hot and it clings to our wet pants and feet, weighing us down. My rubber legs seem separate from my soggy brain, running along to catch up to Foster and Emmett, my arms dead wood at my sides.

When ships land after weeks at sea, the sailors kiss the ground, but I don't want to kiss this ground. This land of color lines and broken promises. It's strange to be in a sea of shirtless brown bodies, like I'm an overexposed photograph, still waiting to develop my color. I wish we were back on the raft, floating to the top of Lake Michigan and on to Canada, where they never even heard of Jim Crow and his stupid rules. We'd put up the tarp. Fish. Stop for water.

On second thought, I wish we were only characters from *Tom Sawyer* and *Huckleberry Finn*. We'd finish the chapter. Close the book. The story'd be over and we'd all go home.

But this is real. Real, unpredictable life full of deadly land mines. It's scary and confusing and my heart is breaking.

Emmett stops in front of a black police officer and explains what happened, and we all charge with him after the lifeguard. As we get closer to Twenty-Ninth Street

Beach, the crowds are even worse and there's a commotion. Lots of men are standing next to their cars, in their straw hats and Sunday shirts and ties, staring intently at the shoreline, scowling.

For a beach that doesn't usually allow any blacks, I see small groups, holding their ground while people shout at them. It's a strange sight.

We all stop on the outskirts of the beach. "What's going on?" Emmett asks the black officer.

"I don't know. Looks like trouble. A fight. A riot, maybe," he answers, and we follow him closer to the beach pavilion, toward a portly white police officer with a sweaty, red face.

The lifeguard we talked to is way ahead of us, and I see him push through the throng of people. He gestures to the Twenty-Ninth Street lifeguard, and both of them jump into a rowboat on the beach. Out on the rocks I see a black man point at something in the lake and a white man diving into the water.

Our officer is arguing with the portly officer on duty here, but the white officer just keeps nodding and throwing up his hands. Their faces are getting closer together.

"These boys are witnesses," says the black officer.

"I didn't see anything. Got enough problems today. With this heat, it's a powder keg."

"It's your duty. Before it's too late. If that boy drowns, it's murder on your watch," the black officer shouts at him.

"Don't advise me of my duty, boy. I tell you, I didn't see anything." The officer pulls his cap low and wipes sweat from his upper lip. His voice is hard and aggravated.

The black officer's nostrils flare and he puts his hands on his billy club. He looks around, as if hoping another officer might be close—another black officer, I figure.

I stand behind Foster and he stands behind Emmett. Emmett's looking away from the policemen, out to the lake, his fists clenched.

"That officer's not going to do anything," Foster whispers to me. "Tell him, Billy. Tell him what happened."

"He's too riled up. It'll make it worse," I whisper back. I think about what Emmett says: "A turtle don't lose his head if he don't stick it out." I ain't worried about losing my head. I swear on the Bible. It's Odell and Emmett and Foster I'm worried about.

"He'll listen to you. Please. Tell him." Foster pulls on my arm to get me to move in front of him, but I don't budge, having trouble thinking straight on account of all the angry yelling around me. What's the right thing to do to keep everybody safe?

"He ain't going to listen to a kid," I say.

But he might, I think. *Because I'm pink with sunburn, just like him. Because we're the same.* But I can't move. No words are forming in my mouth. What's wrong with me? Why don't I step up? What's holding me back?

An angry group of people walk down the beach and form a crowd, blocking us from going toward the water. Two walls of people, one white, one black.

Two lifeguards from Twenty-Ninth Street Beach each have the arm of a man who's giving them some trouble. When they get closer I see the man is Timmy's da, with Timmy tagging along behind. For just the quickest of moments I forget all the hateful things Mr. Beatty's done and instead, just see my best friend's da—and I think, *No matter what angry words he says on the docks, this is different. He'll help us out now, for old time's sake, for loyalty to the Irish. Because "Under the shelter of each other, we survive," like my da says.*

"Mr. Beatty. Mr. Beatty," I say, pushing past Foster.

But in the next second I'm falling into myself, full of horror, because I recognize Timmy's da is wearing the shirt and the hat of the man who threw the rock. It *was* him I saw on the breakwater.

"This is the man they say threw the rock," says the lifeguard. White hands are pulling at Mr. Beatty, but black bodies are pushing him back and penning him in. Timmy is wide-eyed, shivering, his towel over one shoulder.

Mr. Beatty eyes Emmett and Foster, then me. "Go home, Billy," he says coldly. He puts his arm around Timmy's neck. Timmy stares at the ground.

"No, Mr. Beatty. Please."

The black officer moves closer. "Is this the man threw the rock?" he asks us.

Mr. Beatty sneers and leans toward me. "Go home, you N—— lover," he snarls, wrenching his arm free from the lifeguard. He pushes me. I smell the liquor on his breath. Timmy gives me a scared look. A pleading look, and he shakes his head just a notch.

There's a commotion behind Mr. Beatty and we see a body being dragged up onto the breakwater. Emmett pushes past Mr. Beatty to get to the lake. Foster lets out a wail. Without a word, Mr. Beatty swings his fist at Emmett and it bounces off his jaw. Just as Mr. Beatty starts to hit him again, Emmett takes hold of his wrist and stops it midair. Emmett is strong. So strong. He could punch Mr. Beatty back. But he doesn't.

"I just want to help my brother, that's all," I hear him say.

Foster gives me a wild-eyed look.

I point at Mr. Beatty. I yell, "He did it. He threw the rock. I saw him."

Timmy's face contorts into a mask of anger and hate. The black officer motions for the white policeman to help him get Mr. Beatty, but instead the white officer grabs Emmett, pulling his arms back and snapping handcuffs on his wrists.

Foster tilts his head, trying to see the breakwater. He turns to me and cries out, "Is he dead?" I can't answer him before the people push into us.

And in that moment I see the trouble that is coming. I see the hell to pay. It's too hot. People are tired. Tired of fighting for jobs. Tired of being poor. Tired of doing the dirty work. Tired of unwritten rules. Tired of not being equal. And all that tired has turned into hate. *The Chicago Defender* newspaper is right.

"Foster." He doesn't hear me. "Foster," I yell louder, and he turns to me. I reach in my pocket and find my streetcar tokens. I press one into his hand.

"Run," I mouth to him and I point in the opposite direction, knowing that we can't be together.

A freight train is not louder than so many angry people yelling at each other. In a flash I'm past the sand and I've made it to the walkway. I see a black woman slap a white navy officer. I see two white men beating up a black man. I see mothers running with their children, picnic baskets half open with beach blankets dragging.

I look back to the beach from the Thirty-Fifth Street Bridge's walkway. The closest thing I ever seen that compares to this mass of people is the crowd going wild at Comiskey Park, waving caps and shouting. Here, it's a blend of bodies, so close together there's no distinction, like marbled ice cream, chocolate swirling in a sea of vanilla.

This is what my da shuts out with his shell shock. This is what war is. It's confusing. Chaos. It's heart-hammering. I close my eyes and pray again. For my da. For Odell and Emmett and Foster.

Then I run, under the elevated train that rumbles over my head, across street after street, dodging drivers that don't expect to see a boy darting about in front of them. I have to wait for the streetcar on Thirty-First, and by the time it comes I can tell news has spread. Police cars are speeding down the street. I climb up the trolley steps, put my token in the box, and plop down. I'm beet red, I know it. The heat. The shame. The fear. My legs are sticking to the hot leather seat. My brain is jumping helter-skelter around in my head.

Go home? Ma's prolly still busy at the church. Go find

Officer O'Brien? He warned me, didn't he? Go tell Foster's daddy? He doesn't know. Doesn't have any idea of what's happened. Doesn't know the dangerous monster that's rearing its head. It's my fault. Mine. Me, myself, and I.

We bounce to the next stop, and a policeman gets on. I freeze, turning my cheek to the window. He says something to the streetcar driver and hops off.

The next few stops the driver barely waits for new passengers. Once the black passengers are all off the car, he passes all the stops until after Wentworth.

I let my stop go by. I decide what I have to do.

I can see sunbeams flashing between the factories as we bump along up Thirty-First: Dark. Light. Dark. Light. I love the long days of light in the summer. Playing out in the street. Catching fireflies. But now I want night to come. To hide the rottenness, to hide my disgrace. My cowardice.

Something starts to stink when we stop at Racine Avenue, and I know it's The Stock Yard, the smell of rotting death worse in this heat, and I put my hand to my shoulder, on the spot Odell touched when he pushed me down on the raft. It's my fault. My da was wrong when he told me sometimes you got to stand up for what you believe. Look what I done by crossing the line. Look what's come of my grand ideas.

I run up Racine to the bridge and then streak down the bank to Bubbly Creek. Dappled light guides me down the path. I slip and slide and throw myself through the low branches. I feel a pounding in my head with each footstep.

We've been gone all day. I should be starving but my stomach is loose and tight at the same time. Like somebody is cinching a strap around a deflated ball. Is anybody worrying about me? Wondering where I am? Not Ma. She's busy at church, thinking I'm out having a good time with Timmy and Mr. Beatty. Not Mary. She's fixing Da's supper and settling Anna down, thinking I'm taking advantage of my little bit of freedom.

I see the fire pit and the lean-to. What if Foster's daddy ain't here? I got to find him. What if he's still at his sister's in the Black Belt? I got to find him. What if he's out looking for his sons? I got to find him.

But what if I can't? What if I say the wrong thing? What if everything I do makes everything worse? I ain't nothing but a coward.

The fire pit makes a sizzling sound, and I see damp leaves suffocating the glowing embers. I touch the handle of the coffeepot and it's still warm. I squint into the trees. What if they got here first, Mickey or Dynamite Joey or the likes of them? What if . . .

But just then a tall shadow and a small one step from behind the trees.

"Billy," a deep voice declares, sounding rushed and panicked.

"We heard you coming," Foster says. "Sounded like a whole gang of people."

"How did you get here so fast?" I say between breaths.

"I was running for the streetcar and Mr. Montgomery yelled for me to jump up in his wagon with the vegetables. He give me a ride as far as the Pick Factory." In the light I can see white tear streaks on Foster's face.

"Then a police car pulled up next to me on Archer. I was so scared. The officer said, 'You seen Billy? Mr. Weinstein sent me to fetch him home.' When I didn't answer he said, 'There's trouble coming. Stay in the woods. Stay off the streets. If you see Billy tell him to get home quick.'"

"Was it Officer O'Brien? It must have been Officer O'Brien. What'd he say? Did he know anything?" I'm trying to ask about Odell and Emmett, if anybody heard anything, saw anything, but I'm afraid to say it out plain.

Foster knows what I'm trying to ask and shakes his head from side to side. "He don't know anything about Odell. Said he'd go see."

He stares down at the ground and my shoulders start to shake. I can't breathe for the sobs I can't let out.

Mr. Williams touches my shoulder. Right on the same spot where Odell pushed me down with his hand. That does it. I start blubbering like a baby.

"Billy. Son." His voice is deeper and sadder than ever.

"But I—He—We—It—" I can't finish a sentence. I don't have enough air between sobs, and I can't put it into words, anyway.

I want to say . . .

But I didn't mean for anything to happen.

He saved our lives.

We tried to save him.

It shouldn't be like this.

Foster's daddy reaches out his hand to me and I take it. Gently he draws me closer until I'm in the shelter of his arms next to Foster.

We stand there, me gulping, Foster sniffling, Mr. Williams moaning softly. I smell the fire smoke on his arms.

We stand for what feels like a long time, with only the sounds of the woods around us. I wish I could stay here, like this, forever. Not ever having to find out what's happening in the world we ran from.

Mr. Williams breaks the spell. "Billy, I got to go and so do you. I got to find my boys, and you ain't safe here."

I pull away at the same time as Foster, and we both look up at Mr. Williams. His eyes are shiny and full of tears that haven't spilled.

"But it's not fair. We have to get help." I feel so small. So insignificant. So powerless.

Mr. Williams steadies us by laying a hand on the side of each of our arms. "Billy, take the creek path. Foster, stay in the woods, but not by the lean-to. If I'm not back by morning, get to your auntie's house."

"But we have to tell somebody," I start to say. But he's gone, swallowed up by the woods as he heads up the path to Archer Avenue.

I know in my heart I may never see him again—never see any of them again. I know once they get those officers to let Emmett go, once they find Odell—however they find him—they may not feel safe with me again. Or maybe they'll leave Chicago for good.

"Billy?" says Foster, his whisper jolting me from my thoughts.

"What?"

He holds something out to me. It's my knife. And here I thought it was at the bottom of Lake Michigan.

We shake hands. Man to man. Brother to brother. Friend to friend.

"Best friends," Foster whispers.

"Best friends, forever," I whisper back.

Then I run, down the path close to the river this time. I can't help letting out a sob. My heart feels ragged and ripped, but full to overflowing at the same time. I'm almost out of earshot when I hear Foster yell, "Don't fall in the river, Beechnut."

I smile and remember Odell and his stories, and new tears fill up my eyes.

Who's left to tell the stories, I wonder, so full of sadness my feet feel like lead.

I understand so much more now in July than ever I did in February. So much more. How easy it is to be a coward. How hard it is to truly cross the line. How impossible it is to do justice and love mercy.

Chapter Seventeen

I HEAD UP THE ALLEY, keeping clear of the streets. The sky stretches out behind the buildings in sunset colors of pink and peach. I have to get home. My bouncy-ball stomach wobbles as each foot hits the ground and I pound out a prayer with the rhythm.

Let them be okay. Let them be okay. Let them be okay.

I'm just about to zip across the next intersection when a car zooms into view and blocks my way. A police car. Shiny black, CHICAGO POLICE DEPARTMENT in gold letters on the door.

The blood in my pounding head chills and I cling to

the light pole, heaving out breaths. *I'm a goner. Somebody knows what I done.* But then I see Officer O'Brien open the door and step from the car.

"William McDermott, didn't I tell you trouble was coming? I've been down every street three times. Don't you know your mother is worried sick over you? Your boarder come to find me, he did. Told me I might find you down here with your friend."

"Mr. Weinstein went looking for you?" There must be something wrong with my hearing.

"Yes, that's him." Officer O'Brien opens the back door of the car and I step up on the running board and slide in, my legs shaking. Here it is, my first time in a car, a police car no less, but I'm so sick at heart I can't get excited.

Officer O'Brien leans over me. "Billy, stories are flying. Mr. Beatty's been all around town, getting people riled. Saying you're a snake in the grass, a you-know-what lover. And you know Mickey. Full of the temper. Now the Hamburg boys want answers. They're out looking for you." He shuts my door and gets in the other side. "You tell me, Billy. Tell me what happened," he says.

The streetlights haven't come on yet, and the car roof shuts out the sky. He waits before starting the engine. Somewhere a door slams. A dog barks. A porch light winks on. A group of men walk by on the other side of the street. They hold baseball bats like weapons. The bats make me think about my White Sox and I wonder if they got a win today. Then right away I'm sorry to worry about such a thing when so much trouble brews.

Officer O'Brien still waits. I don't know how to start—*where* to start. Mostly I don't know which side he's on, so I don't know what to say. Is he a shelter? Or is he a storm?

"Billy boy," he says in a quieter voice. "You got a scared friend in the woods. And something happened on the beach today. A poor boy's drowned. That boarder of yours, Mr. Weinstein, he explained some things to me. The hate that destroyed his family. The hate that he escaped by coming here." He sighs. "An ugly thing, hate is. I can help you. I want to help you. Your da would want me to."

"My da?" I turn on him and yell, the fear and hurt coming out in anger. "My da? He's no coward. But I'm a coward, d'you hear? A coward. And for nothing. It's over. I didn't take care of my friends. Didn't protect them when I had a chance. If my da even knew," I start to bawl.

"Okay, Billy, it's okay." He pats my shaking knee. "Just tell me. We'll sort it out, won't we? Maybe we just got to hear the story to understand."

And then I know. Just like my da always told me I

would. Who's left to tell the stories? I'm left. It's up to me. To tell it like Odell would tell it. To tell it like Foster would want me to. And to tell it so the monsters in Mr. Williams's newspaper articles can't blot out all the justice and mercy in the world.

I start from the beginning, at James Ward. From me being new and Foster being my friend, playing stickball with me, inviting me to see the fort. I tell about Tom Sawyer and Huck Finn, and Foster's idea to build a raft and how the Williamses can't swim. I tell about Mickey and Joey hurting that little boy and his puppy, and how Mickey threatened my family.

I hardly take a breath. Everything pours out. How I went to warn Foster and found out the lean-to wasn't a fort, but their home. How I started reading *The Chicago Defender*, learning about lynchings and riots. I describe all the Williamses. Smart and inventing Emmett, never wanting trouble. Strong and sensitive Odell with his funny stories. Loyal and considerate Foster, my best friend, who almost got hanged when I dragged him to see the White Sox.

Then I tell about today. Start to finish. I start to cry softly when I tell about Odell pushing Foster and me down and getting hit with the rock, but then my anger boils right up over the tears as I finish telling about the horror. "No one helped. Mr. Beatty pushed me back. He pushed me. And he slugged Emmett. And that fat, white policeman arrested Emmett instead of Mr. Beatty. I tried to tell him who done it, but he didn't listen to me. He didn't listen." I heave a big sigh. My knees aren't knocking anymore, but my heart is still pounding. "Then me and Foster, we run away, just like sissies."

Officer O'Brien starts the car. "You're not a coward for running from a fight, Billy. Not from a fight that could kill you. Better to be a chicken for one minute than dead for the rest of your life." He pulls off the brake and the car moves forward. "Those bloody fools on the beach. They think they're tough. Well, every hard-boiled egg is yellow inside."

"But my da stands up for what he believes. He told me."

"He learned to stand up, Billy, just like you're learning. Just like you did today, standing up to tell who done it and telling me the story of what happened. Sure, and we're all still learning, now, even the likes of me." He sighs and taps his chest.

"I never knew it would come to this. I should of set Mickey straight, but I just thought he was blowing off steam. I never thought he'd do these things, I swear I didn't." His voice gets louder and he slaps the side of his leg with the palm of his hand.

"Let me see what I can do. See what I can find out about Odell. Put things right with the brother that's arrested. I know the officers on that beat. Let me do that for you and your family."

We pull out onto Archer. The streetcars are gone. And the streetlights are on now, bugs swarming around them like the people on the beach today around the officers. We pull alongside a horse and wagon. A boy is driving, He's Emmett's size, but darker in color.

We both look over in the wagon and see a man in it, laying very still, a blanket wrapped around his chest. Open crates of produce surround him. I recognize the wagon.

"That's Mr. Montgomery," I tell Officer O'Brien. "He helped Foster get to the woods."

Mr. O'Brien glances at the wagon and then looks at me, long and hard. He takes a deep breath and lets it out slow, like a strong man setting down a two-hundred-pound weight.

"Sonny," Officer O'Brien yells out his window. "Best get off the street."

The boy brings the wagon to a complete stop. "I will, Officer. Soon as I get my uncle to Provident Hospital."

Officer O'Brien asks, "What's happened?"

"A mob pulled him right out of our wagon. Beat him up for nothing. Nothing." The boy starts to choke up, and I see his hands tighten on the reins.

Officer O'Brien shakes his head. "Bloody fools. No good will come tonight."

He shouts back at the boy. "You go on. Don't go down Thirty-Fifth or Wentworth. Head up Halsted to Twenty-Sixth. Then turn right and go to Dearborn. After I see to this one, I'll follow you. Make sure there's no more trouble."

Poor Mr. Montgomery. Just trying to make a living for himself and his family with his produce wagon. If he was born a white man, he'd be the grocer at the Bridgeport Market, safe at home right now seeing as how they're not even open on Sundays. That big word, disenfranchisement, comes haunting me again. It's a big word for a big problem that's not only down in the South, but right here in the North, in big-city Chicago.

The boy flicks the reins and Officer O'Brien touches the gas pedal. We're much faster than the wagon, and I turn my head and watch the boy until I can't see him anymore. Before I know it, we're on my street and in front of my house. A classy tin lizzie is parked right smack dab at the bottom of the stairs to my flat. *Must be somebody having a fancy visitor, driving a Ford Model T like that,* I think.

Officer O'Brien opens my door and I jump down. He follows me up the stairs. Before we're halfway up, the door flies open and Ma comes screaming out at me.

"William Jarlath McDermott. Saints alive. For the love of God, where've you been? You've just about killed your poor mother."

First she kisses both of my cheeks and squeezes me tight, then she wallops me on the behind, pushing me ahead of her while she holds her hand out to Officer O'Brien. "How can we ever thank you, Michael? May the Lord bless you."

Officer O'Brien speaks softly to Ma so I can't hear as I climb the steps ahead of them. Then he calls out, "You keep out of trouble, Billy boy." I hear his car rumble off as I open the door to my house.

At least, I think it's my house. But there's a man sitting in my da's chair and Mr. Weinstein is pacing up and down in the hallway. Sets of suitcases stand like soldiers along the wall and the hall closet is open and empty, except for Da's uniform and Ma's fur. Mary is weeping. Anna's eyes are bigger than a half-dollar and she's sucking her thumb. Ma doesn't even tell her to stop.

Everyone turns to stare at me when I walk into the front room.

"Ma?" I turn to look at her face. Then I scan the room again. I don't see Da. Did something happen to Da? "Ma?" I yell and I grab for her.

Mr. Weinstein holds up his hand. In his thick accent he says, "There's nothing to worry about. Nothing."

Ma shuts the door and locks it. "We're leaving, Billy. Da's already at the train station with the rest of our things. Mary packed up some of your things. Go finish."

"But—"

Ma whirls on me. "And I should explain things to you after Mrs. Beatty had to come explaining things to me about my very own boy? You, lying to me all these weeks? You, who doesn't tell a body where you're going? You, who could be floating dead in Lake Michigan right now?"

I close my mouth and slink down the hall to our bedroom. Ma hardly ever speaks crossly to me, and I'm ashamed I made her so sick with worry.

But where are we going? And why? Who's the man in the front room?

I can hear Mary begging Ma, "Please let me stay. Please. I can work for my room and board at the Dolans'."

"That's what you want, is it, Miss Mary? So you can

sneak off with your fellow whenever you like? Oh, Mrs. Beatty had plenty to tell me about you, too. Plenty. Bless her meddling, but she had to, didn't she? Swallow my pride, I did. Jaysus, Mary, and the martyrs."

Mary wails and flies down the hall and into the bedroom.

"It's all your fault," she says to me. "I will hate you forever."

"Why? What's happening?"

Mary launches into an outburst, and the whole story comes out. Timmy ran to the parish and told his Ma everything about me and the Williams and the raft and Odell and Emmett. I guess he even told his Ma about Mary and Joey being sweet on each other. Then Mrs. Beatty rushed to tell Ma. And Ma told Mr. Weinstein, and he went and got Officer O'Brien to make sure I was safe.

"It's not safe for us here. That's what Officer O'Brien said. Not safe. They're looking for you, Billy. Mickey and his boys. And what's Da going to do? They hate us now. And Joey will hate me, too." She's still crying, but softer.

"But Mary, you weren't at the beach. You didn't see what happened. Mr. Beatty tried to hurt me and my friends, for no reason. We're no scabs. We didn't steal jobs. It ain't fair, Mary. It ain't right."

It's like she can't hear me. She just keeps talking. "Mr.

Weinstein got his friend to bring a car for Da. He paid for train tickets for us. All of us. We've been throwing things in suitcases for hours."

"Where? Where are we going?"

"To Uncle Sid and Aunt Ava's. In Detro-o-oit." She stretches out Detroit, like it's the end of the world.

I'm madly emptying the drawer in the dresser we share, throwing my cards and marbles into a sack and stuffing my school pants and shirts, and my baseball glove and ball into a suitcase. I fish my knife from my pocket and almost toss it in, too, but then I decide it might come in handy on the train and put it back in my pocket. I lift up the mattress and grab my stack of *Chicago Defender* newspapers.

Mary gasps. "Billy, what're you doing with that garbage?"

I lay the newspapers over my clothes and snap the suitcase shut. "Did you ever think maybe Joey is wrong? Did you ever think maybe there's not just one way of thinking? Remember what Da told us, Mary. Don't judge a book by the cover. Don't you ever think about that? Don't you think about standing up for what's right?"

I drag my suitcase down the hall. We're leaving Chicago? I can't even picture it. I only ever lived in Chicago. When will we be back? What if the White Sox go to the World Series without me, their number one fan?

We're a family of cowards, that's what we are. Running off scared, tails between our legs. Running from a fight.

But maybe my family can't survive this fight. Maybe it's okay to be a quitter if it saves lives. Better to be a chicken for one minute than dead for the rest of your life. That's what Officer O'Brien said. Maybe someday my da can explain it to me.

Ma stands in her fur, holding the picnic basket, talking to Mr. Weinstein. Ninety degrees and she's wearing her fur.

"Yes. Yes. It vill be done," he's saying. "I vill tell you, to this address. I vill send to you." Hearing the way he says "will" makes me smile, and I get choked up thinking I'll miss him and his funny ways. He waves the slip of paper. Then he sees me and puts his hand on my shoulder. "It vill be all right. I too survive this. Leave my country to be safe. Leave to live."

I touch his sleeve. "What happened to the others?"

"What others?" he asks.

"The others that stayed. The ones who didn't leave."

He shakes his head. "There are no more others."

We march through the front room and toward the door. Mr. Weinstein's friend, the driver, carries the two big suitcases. Ma holds Anna's hand.

Mary comes up behind me. She whispers, still crying a

little, "I do think about Da, Billy. I do think about what's right. But it's different for a girl. Not safe. Da can't protect me. Not like Joey can."

I whisper back. "I will, Mary. I'll protect you." I find her hand with my empty one and give it a quick squeeze.

"I know you vill," she says, pronouncing "will" just like Mr. Weinstein, and we both tilt our mouths up in little smiles.

"Billy," Ma says over her shoulder. "Carry Da's uniform. Don't let it drag."

I get to the bottom of the stairs and I stop. I look around. My heart is breaking. This is my home and I'm leaving. I'm stealing away in the middle of the night like a no-count weasel. I get a lump the size of a baseball in my throat and water in my eyes.

And then that baseball lump gives me an idea. I throw Da's uniform over the stair railing, put my suitcase down on the ground, and rustle around under the *Chicago Defender* newspapers.

"Billy, saints alive, what're you doing?" Ma says in as loud a voice as she dares.

Everybody is scrambling into the car. I find my glove, my da's lucky glove, and my baseball, and I run over to our secret hiding spot.

"Come on, Billy, come on," Mary hisses.

I pull the stone from the secret hiding space and carefully put my baseball into the center of my glove. I take my knife from my pocket and poke the point into my finger, then press the dot of blood onto the ball. I shove it as far down in the hole as it will go. I whisper, "Take care of my glove, Foster," and kiss the stone before I slide it back—for luck, just like we do the paver at Comiskey Park.

When I stand up, Mr. Weinstein is right behind me and I jump about a mile.

"For your friend, no?" he asks in his Russian accent.

I nod. "For my friend."

"I watch. If he no come. I take to him," he says.

"But you don't—" I start to say.

Mr. Weinstein is already heading to the car, but he turns and gives me a look that sees straight to my heart. "You not only spy in this house." And he winks. "We are the same, no? We have secrets. We have stories to tell. If we are brave to tell them."

And I sure don't expect Mr. Weinstein to be on my side, but then, ain't I been saying that life is unpredictable?

"Tell him his blood brother will come back someday," I say. "We'll make it better together."

And we walk to the car side by side.

Author's Note

WHILE RIDING BIKES ALONG CHICAGO'S lakefront, my husband and I stopped to read a memorial marker dedicated to Eugene Williams. Eugene was killed by a rock thrown from the breakwater because his raft crossed the invisible racial color line between beaches on July 27, 1919. Chicago's worst race riot started with that incident, although trouble had been simmering long before that. Visit my website, BibiBelford.com, for some historical facts from this time period.

Billy is just a character in a book. But his battle with racism is something every person wrestles with, in one way or another. The monster of prejudice still hasn't been crushed despite our many laws of protection, continued protests and speeches, and heartbreaking sacrifices. Technology allows us to witness its ugliness. And as witnesses, what should be our response?

One of the beta readers for this manuscript believes dialogue brings understanding. Writing this book opened doors to dialogue for me, challenging me to confront my perspectives.

My heart breaks for people who experience discrimination and prejudice. Our cultures, backgrounds, and circumstances may be different, but we are all capable of showing our respect for human life with kindness and tolerance.

In the end I believe Micah 6:8 gives me guidance: "You must act with justice. You must love to show mercy. And you must be humble as you live in the sight of your God." (NIrV)

This is a work of fiction based on a historical event, and to the best of my ability, I've tried to accurately research the time period while still being sensitive to the vocabulary that is considered kind today.

My only goals in writing this book are to honor the memory of Eugene Williams, and to challenge readers to cross the line and live under the shelter of each other.

Acknowledgments

A LAKE FRONT BIKE PATH. A stone memorial. A moment in history. The intersection of these three things inspired me to write the novel *Crossing the Line*.

Eugene Williams lost his life in 1919 from a violent act born out of racism, but even as I began to write the story in 2015, violence continued to escalate in our country, with over 12,500 hate crimes, 57 percent racially motivated, and most of those against African Americans, specifically males under twenty-four years old. My more privileged experience as a white person hadn't prepared me to agonize about the lifespan of young black lives, and I worried for those I knew and loved.

I decided I wasn't qualified to write a novel about racism at such a time, but encouragement came from some amazing women who prayed for me and cheered me on. You know who you are: MC, AN, SP, CF, AM, AV, LR, EO.

During the process of writing *Crossing the Line*, I read two eye-opening books: *Small Great Things* by Jodi Picoult, and *Underground Railroad* by Colson Whitehead. I thank those authors for their craft and for educating my ignorance.

It's not possible to get first person accounts of what happened in 1919, but while researching, I hired a motorboat driver, Sean Biggins, and we searched the river until we found waterways that might have existed back then. I also attended a Chicago Loop Bridges Tour, http://chicagoloopbridges.com, and Jim Phillips shared his expertise on the historic bridges over the Chicago River. On a Chicago Ghost Tour, freetoursbyfoot.com, Andy Meholick enlightened me with some little-known Chicago ghost history as we explored the sites of Chicago's historic disasters. All of these experiences helped my imagination recreate what may have happened during the summer of 1919.

The final stages of editing my manuscript into book shape happened because of revision decisions, proposed by my editor Rachel Stark, whose keen eye and tenacious questioning hopefully ferreted out most inaccuracies. And who knew that words like babysit and stink-eye weren't used in 1919? Thank goodness author Randall Platt knew, and I owe a huge heap of gratitude for her generous application of historical accuracy to my phrasing and word choice.

And then I sought feedback before publication from generous readers, willing to critique and comment. Beta readers: Elizabeth Eisenman, fifth grade teacher at Allen School, and her fifth grade students, Nick Byrnes, Jayda Hughlett, David Marek, Ricardo Millan, Kaya Paetzold, and Jalen Sims. Sensitivity readers: Donnell Collins, Juanita L. Henry, Robbie Booth, and Ray Hull. And of course, Shaw Belford, my husband.

Thank you all for everything. I truly do live in the shelter of you.